"He's terri[...]

"But what?"

Cheryl grimaced, trying [...] Did they really matter? "He won't last a month."

Robyn's eyebrows shot up. "Why do you say that? So far, he loves it here."

darling baby boy, she valued her family above all else.

Polar opposites.

SUSAN PAGE DAVIS and her husband, Jim, have been married thirty-four years and have six children, ages fifteen to thirty-two, and six grandchildren. They live in Maine, where they are active in a small, independent Baptist church. Susan is a homeschooling mother. She has published more than twenty novels in the historical romance, cozy mystery, romantic suspense, fantasy, and contemporary genres. She loves to hear from her readers. Visit Susan at her Web site: www.susanpagedavis.com.

Books by Susan Page Davis

HEARTSONG PRESENTS

HP607—Protecting Amy
HP692—Oregon Escort
HP708—The Prisoner's Wife
HP719—Weaving a Future
HP727—Wyoming Hoofbeats
HP739—The Castaway's Bride
HP756—The Lumberjack's Lady
HP800—Return to Love
HP811—A New Joy
HP827—Abiding Peace
HP850—Trail to Justice
HP865—Always Ready
HP881—Fire and Ice

Don't miss out on any of our super romances. Write to us at the following address for information on our newest releases and club information.

Heartsong Presents Readers' Service
PO Box 721
Uhrichsville, OH 44683

Or visit www.heartsongpresents.com

Polar
Opposites

Susan Page Davis

Heartsong Presents

To my newest grandchild, Abigail Faith, I can't wait to get to know you.

A note from the Author:
I love to hear from my readers! You may correspond with me by writing:

Susan P. Davis
Author Relations
PO Box 721
Uhrichsville, OH 44683

ISBN 978-1-60260-778-1

POLAR OPPOSITES

Our mission is to publish and distribute inspirational products offering exceptional value and biblical encouragement to the masses.

PRINTED IN THE U.S.A.

one

Cheryl Holland left her car in short-term parking at the Anchorage airport and hurried toward the terminal, zipping her jacket. Late October winds held a biting promise of snow.

She wished she'd asked her son-in-law for a photo of the passenger she was supposed to pick up. But an emergency call had come in, and Rick had rushed out the door of the veterinary hospital calling over his shoulder, "Oh, Cheryl, I'm supposed to pick Oz up at eleven. Can you possibly. . . ?"

"Sure," she'd called blithely. In the past year, she'd become Rick's right-hand man, gal Friday, and jack-of-all-trades, rolled into one. And she loved it. But it would be nice to know what the new veterinary partner looked like.

"Maybe he'll carry his instruments in a medical bag like Rick's." She strode past the airline check-in areas and a gift shop selling Native Alaskan art. "Great. Now I'm talking to myself." A woman heading the other way eyed her cautiously, and Cheryl smiled. "Hello." *Note to self*, she thought. *Don't talk to yourself in public.*

She paused below a flight board and searched for Oz Thormond's flight from Seattle. At least she'd found the number scrawled on Rick's notepad. The one thing she knew about Dr. Thormond's appearance was that he would look nothing like the young veterinarian whose photo she had posted on the Baker Animal Hospital's Web site a month ago. That was Dr. Brad Irwin, the new vet school grad Rick had hired to work with him and possibly become a partner in the business. The same bright-eyed young veterinarian who had decided at the

5

last possible minute that he didn't want to live in Alaska after all and had walked away from the job offer.

Cheryl still steamed about that. She'd worried a little about Dr. Irwin's youth and inexperience, but Rick had reminded her that he couldn't pay a lot at first. As the practice continued to expand, he would raise Dr. Irwin's salary. She'd also cautioned him that the young man from North Carolina might find Alaska a little overwhelming. And cold.

Rick had scoffed.

Until Brad Irwin had dumped the job offer with no warning.

"That's right," Cheryl said. "I hinted that he ought to have made the guy sign a contract, too. My son-in-law is entirely too trusting."

A man searching the Arrivals board shot her a sidelong glance. Cheryl favored him with a cheery smile and a bright, "Hello. Sorry about that."

"No problem. My son-in-law's not the greatest either."

She laughed. "Oh, Rick's terrific. But he assumes everyone else is as honorable as he is." She spotted the number for Dr. Thormond's flight. On time and landing in ten minutes. The baggage claim area would be the place to find him. She smiled at the disgruntled father-in-law and walked away.

Okay, no more talking to myself. I'm looking for a man who graduated from vet school with Rick, so probably early thirties. She smiled as she remembered Rick's euphoria when he'd learned Oz would come.

"Cheryl, this is fantastic! I told you that I asked my friend last summer to come work with me, and he couldn't. He was all tied up doing bear research at zoos in the Lower 48. Well, guess what? He's got a grant to come to Alaska and take part in a polar bear project on the North Slope. And when he's not doing that, he wants to live here in Wasilla and join my practice. My first pick for partners, and he's actually coming."

Her daughter, Robyn, had been as overjoyed as Rick, and

the two of them had quickly adjusted their plans. Cheryl had promptly deleted Dr. Irwin's photo and bio from the Web site, but Rick gave her nothing with which to replace it.

"It's happening so fast, he probably doesn't have time to do that. He's moving up here in two weeks. We'll get the info from him when he gets here."

She'd had to be satisfied with that. On the home page of the site, she posted a banner announcing Dr. Oswald Thormond's imminent arrival, all the time wondering if this new arrangement would fall through, too.

She found a vacant seat between two deserted baggage carousels for Alaska Airlines and pulled out her cell phone.

Rick answered her call immediately.

"I'm at the airport, in baggage claim. How will I know this guy?"

Rick laughed. "He'll be the one with the wide-eyed stare and the big grin. Blue eyes and— Oops, gotta go. Sorry, Cheryl."

She considered making a Dr. Thormond sign to hold up, but she had no materials. Passengers began filtering into the area from the gates above. She scrutinized each man who entered. They all clustered around the nearest carousel. Within five minutes, fifty or sixty people had gathered. A digital sign over the farther carousel flashed to life, declaring, Seattle AA flight 5790. As a group, the passengers moved over to the second carousel.

Cheryl eliminated anyone who was not traveling alone or had been met by someone else. She spotted a sober young man with glasses and a moustache on the other side of the moving belt. Possibility. She watched him closely as suitcases began flowing along the carousel. He had a wheeled carry-on and a soft briefcase that might hold a laptop, and he now waited for checked bags. Time to approach him.

She sucked in a deep breath and rose. Before she could push her way to his side, the young man hauled a huge camouflage bag off the belt. She quickly skirted the crowd. When she was halfway around, she saw him exiting toward the parking lot. Okay. So that wasn't him. Disappointed and less confident than before, if possible, she turned back and stood at the edge of the crowd, seeking a man who was looking for someone. After all, Oz would expect Rick to be here, and he'd search the crowd for him, wouldn't he?

A rugged young man in camouflage pants and a hooded sweatshirt stood alone but periodically scanned the crowd. But he was too young. Wasn't he? She wavered. Maybe he had a boyish face for his age.

Blue eyes, Rick had said. She'd have to get closer to be sure.

She edged around the people who huddled three deep about the loop of the carousel, losing sight of her quarry for a moment. When she spotted him again, she was within a few yards, but he was turned away, arranging his carry-on atop the large suitcase he'd just retrieved.

Cheryl walked closer and cleared her throat. "Dr. Thormond?"

He ignored her, struggling with the strap to his smaller bag.

"Excuse me," she said louder. "Are you—"

He looked up at her with curious and very brown eyes.

"I'm sorry. You're not Dr. Thormond, are you?"

"I wish. I've got two more years of med school." He straightened and gave her a pleasant nod then turned toward the exit.

Cheryl sighed and let her posture droop. Maybe she should just wait until the crowd dissipated and see who was left.

She started back to the set of chairs, but a couple with two young children had claimed them. Instead, Cheryl shrank back toward a wall of brochures touting local attractions and again scanned the travelers.

One in particular caught her eye, but not because he was a young, hip veterinarian. The gentleman—and Cheryl knew instinctively that he *was* a gentleman from his bearing and the way he courteously worked his way through other passengers to the conveyor—looked about fifty, with wings of white accenting the lush, dark hair at his temples. She watched him covertly as he set down his carry-on bag and swung a large wheeled suitcase off the belt. He waited for another, giving her the opportunity to study him further. He was just too handsome. *If only,* she thought.

She made herself search again for a much younger man. Blue eyes…early thirties… No one of that description leaped out at her. Edging around behind the crowd, she realized she neared the handsome man's position. Oops. No thirty-somethings over here. She'd better turn back.

Before she could act on the thought, the people parted and the man she'd admired from a distance halted two steps from her. "Sorry," he said with a smile.

She couldn't help staring up into his vibrant, very blue eyes. "Oh, excuse me." She stepped quickly to one side.

He nodded. "Thanks. I'll just get this mountain of baggage out of the way while I wait for my ride."

He parked himself nearby and looked over the heads of the thinning throng. After five minutes or so, only a dozen travelers were left. Cheryl was very aware of the man still waiting patiently with his bags. She glanced over at him and he smiled.

"I suppose I should have the person I'm meeting paged," she said.

"That's an idea. I could ask them to page my friend, too. Rick was always punctual in school. He must have had an emergency."

Cheryl froze, her stomach doing an odd flip. "Rick? Not Rick Baker?"

The man focused on her and nodded. "Yes, actually."

She felt a flush wash over her cheeks. "You must be Dr. Thormond."

"Yes, I. . ." He smiled and held out his hand. "If I'm not mistaken, we're waiting for each other."

"I'm Cheryl Holland, Rick's mother-in-law. And you're right.

He did have an emergency this morning."

The gentleman shook her hand and held on to it, gazing into her eyes. His dark eyebrows drew together. "No. You can't be. Rick's *mother-in-law*? Absolutely impossible."

Cheryl stepped back, releasing his hand. "Oh, I assure you it's true. Rick married my daughter, Robyn, last summer, and—"

"Yes, yes, Robyn. I've heard all about her and her sled dog business. Sorry I couldn't make the wedding. But. . ." He eyed her, cocking his head a little to one side. "Pardon my astonishment, but I'm finding it hard to believe you're old enough to be Rick's mother-in-law."

After the split second it took to absorb that, coming from the lips of a devastatingly handsome man in her own age bracket, Cheryl laughed. "I can see we're going to have an interesting time of it at the practice."

"Are we?" he asked.

"Yes. You see, I'm not only Rick's mother-in-law, I'm his receptionist and aide-de-camp."

His tentative smile broadened. "I must say, I like the way things are shaping up."

She couldn't look into those twinkling eyes any longer. In the four years since Dan Holland died, she hadn't engaged in a single conversation she would consider flirtatious. It felt good in a way—exciting, affirming that she hadn't become a shriveled old widow. But a few moments' banter was one thing. Did she expect an ongoing flirtation in the office? That was the furthest thing from her desire. Time to establish a more professional relationship if she intended to work with this man on a daily basis.

"Well, Dr. Thormond, if you have all your bags, let me help you get them to my car. The drive to Wasilla takes forty-five minutes or so. Did they feed you on the plane?"

"No, I slept most of the way from Seattle. I don't suppose there's a café where we could stop on the way?"

Cheryl laughed. "There's a wide variety of restaurants, sir. Anything from burgers to Thai food. I even know a place famous for Alaskan dishes—sourdough biscuits and reindeer sausage."

He raised one hand to his heart. "That sounds wonderful, but I doubt we could properly appreciate a place like that in less than a couple of hours. Perhaps we'd better stick with something quick and directly on our path. I'm good for Thai food, if you are."

"Excellent choice. We pass right by a good place."

Cheryl insisted on taking one of his smaller bags, and they wended their way out to the short-term parking lot.

"I thought about renting a car right away, but Rick advised me to wait. Said he's got a vehicle I can use for a few weeks until I get my feet under me and see what I want."

"Probably my daughter's Jeep. I think that's wise. Rick has a pickup, completely stocked with his veterinary equipment. You may want to get a similar rig eventually."

They reached her car, and she unlocked the trunk. While Dr. Thormond lifted his bags into it, she reminded herself again that today was the day to set the tone for her working relationship with him. "Professional," she said under her breath.

"Excuse me?" His eyebrows arched, and his lips quirked, just waiting to smile again.

"Nothing. Sorry." She quickly unlocked the doors and slid into the driver's seat, telling herself silently, *And no more talking to yourself, Cheryl. That's an order.*

બ

Oz faced Cheryl Holland across the table at the restaurant, and two things struck him at once. He was very hungry, and she had a shy streak. The hunger issue had been addressed, and their orders would arrive in a few minutes. As to her reserve, she seemed friendly enough, but she had trouble making eye contact now that they were seated close together, face-to-face. Just a matter of drawing her out, he supposed.

"So, tell me about the rental cabin Rick found for me to

stay at. Have you seen it?"

"Yes. In fact, we had it ready for. . ." Her face went a becoming pink. "I'm sorry, this is a little embarrassing. But you know we had another veterinarian lined up for this position?"

"Oh yes, Rick told me about it. He asked me to join him way back last summer. At the time, that looked impossible. So he went ahead and hired someone else. Then the guy ran out on him."

"Right. I just. . .didn't want you to think you were our second choice or anything. Rick wanted you from the start, but when that couldn't happen, he hired this Dr. Irwin. We found housing for him and did a lot to prepare for his arrival. Rick was very disappointed when he backed out—we all were. But then we prayed about it together. The next day Rick told me he'd called you to get your advice and you were considering coming to Wasilla after all."

"Not often we get a second chance at an opportunity we've muffed." Oz watched the change in her face as she warmed to the topic. Cheryl animated was well worth watching. He smiled at her. "This is going to be a great adventure. Rick and I got along famously in school, and I'd give up a lot for the chance to work with him. But to do that *and* have the ability to do polar bear research. . .well, it's a dream come true for me."

Cheryl smiled back. She'd definitely relaxed a bit. "I admit I was surprised when I first realized *you* were Dr. Thormond. I expected a younger man—someone Rick's age. He didn't have a photo, and he hadn't described you very well."

Oz chuckled. "I went back to school and began the career I'd really wanted for twenty years."

"That's wonderful. What did you do before vet school?"

"I was in corrections."

Her jaw dropped, but she recovered quickly. "Prison work?"

"That's right. It started out as an expedient course of action. My father died, leaving my mother destitute. I took the job that would pay me the most short-term—as a guard at the county jail. I'd finished college, but not grad school. I gave up the dream for two decades."

The waitress brought their plates and they looked at each other.

"I'm guessing you're a lady who prays before she eats."

Cheryl's soft brown eyes widened. "Well, yes, I am."

Oz chuckled. "Rick wouldn't marry a woman who wasn't a genuine believer, and I figured the chances were good that her mom was, too. Shall we?"

They bowed their heads, and Oz offered a brief blessing for the meal and thanks for his safe journey. When he looked up, Cheryl's face was pensive as she spread her napkin in her lap. The spicy smell of ginger and cashew chicken made his mouth water, and he reached for his fork.

"You stayed in corrections for twenty years?" she asked.

"Nearly. I went from the county jail to a federal facility, where I eventually became a supervisor. But even though I wasn't one of the inmates, I felt the confinement. Wanted to get outside more. And I'd dreamed of working with animals since I was a kid. Working with the prisoners gave me a measure of satisfaction—I was giving back to the community, so to speak. But it wore me down emotionally. Made me cynical."

"I suppose it would."

"It struck me that it wasn't too late to go to grad school and get the credentials. That was about twelve years ago, and I've never looked back."

Cheryl smiled and gave a little nod, as though his explanation satisfied her doubts. "Working with animals is very therapeutic. It kept our whole family going after my husband died."

"In what way?" Oz asked softly, aware that he was getting a peek behind Cheryl's outward demeanor. She'd represented the veterinary practice so far today, but this was personal.

"Robyn and I—and my father-in-law, too—were devastated

when Dan died. My son, Aven, is a Coast Guard officer. Of course, he came home on leave. But after Aven went back to his ship, Robyn and Steve and I sat down and made plans. My husband had worked for an oil company, and he drew a good salary. Without that, we had to support ourselves. We decided to build the kennel—which had been more or less a hobby—into a first-class business. Robyn trains sled teams for the best now, and world-class racers are buying Holland Kennel puppies."

"Rick's told me a little about it. He's really proud of her."

"Yes. I took a part-time job outside, but we got by, and now the business is something we're all proud of." They ate in silence, but a few minutes later, she lifted her teacup and looked at him over the rim. "I'd love to hear more about your bear research."

He liked her unaffected friendliness, and even her slight reserve. She showed the interest that made a good listener. Instinct told him she was good at her job and Rick's office ran smoothly. Alaska looked better and better.

"I've spent the last three years doing bear research at zoos," he said. "Polar bears have always intrigued me, and they're very different from other species. I've traveled to northern Canada and Siberia to study bear populations. This year I applied for a couple of programs, and what do you know? The Alaska Department of Fish and Wildlife contracted me to do wildlife research in February, and I'll go out with a team of geologists on a privately funded trip at the end of March."

"Wonderful."

"I'm excited about it. After I got that news, Rick contacted me again with his offer. He says he can give me time off from the practice to continue my research, so I jumped at it."

"I'm glad you have a chance to follow your passion."

"Yes, and earn a living, too." Oz laughed and took a sip of his coffee. "I can hardly wait to get up to the North Slope."

"Would you like dessert?"

They both looked up at the waitress.

"What do you say?" Oz raised his eyebrows and smiled at Cheryl.

"Not for me, thanks, but go ahead if you'd like."

"I guess we're all set," he told the waitress. He reached for his wallet.

"Oh, this is a business expense," Cheryl said. "Rick told me to put it on the credit card for the practice."

"We have a credit card for the vet practice?"

She laughed at his expression. "I guess we're not quite as primitive as you thought."

"To be frank, I figured Rick was broke. He told me about the new building and everything."

"You'll love it. And he did take some loans for that, but our receipts are good. I'm sure you'll want to discuss the details with him, but I can tell you that he doesn't seem worried about his financial future. Which is nice for me, as an employee and a mother-in-law. We're all proud of the way he's built the business."

"I can't wait to see it." Oz pushed his chair back. "Shall we?"

They went to the car, and Cheryl put the key in the ignition. No response came from the engine.

Her face fell. "Hold on."

"Flat battery?" Oz asked.

She reached down and fumbled on the floor beneath her seat then opened her door. "No, this happens all the time. I can fix it." She pulled a lever to pop the hood and climbed out.

Oz wondered if he should offer to call a service station.

Metallic tapping came from beyond the raised hood. Cheryl lowered it with a thud and got in. When she turned the key, the engine roared to life. She smiled at him apologetically. "I really need to go at those terminals with a wire brush. They're quite corroded." She put the gear shift into reverse. "I guess I know what I'll be doing after supper tonight. Sorry about that."

Oz couldn't think of a suitable reply, so he sat back and

admired the scenery. Mountains towered in the distance to his right, and as Cheryl headed out of the city, ranks of peaks unfolded in the distance. He'd heard so much about Alaska, but the reality dwarfed all the tales. Already he knew he would love the land. A tiny, rodent-like anxiety gnawed at his satisfaction. What about the twenty-hour nights in winter and the sub-zero temperatures for weeks on end?

"I hope you like your cabin." Cheryl pushed back her short, curly hair and shot him a sideways glance. "It's only big enough for one person, but I suppose it will do until you find something better."

"I'm sure I'll find it suitably rustic, yet comfortable." He grinned at her, and she smiled back.

He was really here, in the land of glaciers, dog sleds, and women who fixed their own cars. That flutter of doubt had shadowed him since he'd accepted Rick's invitation two weeks ago, but he'd never faced it head-on. He didn't intend to either. The adventure was on.

two

Cheryl tried to concentrate on her work the next morning, but that was difficult, knowing Oz Thormond was touring the Baker Animal Hospital with Rick as his guide. Whenever they entered the hall, she could hear their deep voices. Oz's enthusiastic laugh punctuated Rick's account of his headaches while seeing the new facility built.

The front door opened, and Cheryl turned toward it, expecting a pet owner with an unscheduled patient in need of medical care.

Instead, Robyn walked in. "Hi, Mom! How's it going?"

"Terrific. Dr. Thormond seems impressed."

"Isn't he great? I like him a lot." Robyn's dark eyes danced. "He and Rick spent the evening catching up and telling me tales about their days in vet school. Sounds as though those two had as much fun as a couple of kids in an amusement park."

"Really? Rick strikes me as a serious young man, although I know he has a playful side." She tried to imagine Oz Thormond pulling practical jokes and cutting up. She shook her head. "I like Dr. Thormond, too, but I don't see him as a delinquent. He was at the top of their class, Rick tells me."

"He's smart all right. I didn't mean that they did anything awful. But together, they seem to enjoy life more than the average person does."

"Hmm. Maybe it's not such a good idea for them to work together."

"Are you kidding?" Robyn perched on the corner of Cheryl's desk. "They'll get twice the work done, with half the stress.

17

You'll see."

"Yes, I will." Cheryl decided not to mention the added stress she felt whenever Oz's laughing blue eyes settled on her. The very thought sent an unwelcome warmth to her cheeks, and she shoved her wheeled chair back and stood. "So, what are you here for, young lady?"

"I'm going out to a kennel with Rick this morning."

"Oh yes, the Bensons'. He's going to vaccinate two litters of puppies and check a dog that we had in here last month with a fractured tibia."

"Right. Ron Benson has a breeding female shepherd for sale, and I thought I'd take a look."

"You'd add a German shepherd to your breeding stock? Since when?"

"Oh, I don't expect to buy her. But I haven't had much time with Rick this week, and it'll be fun to ride along with him. Besides, I called Grandpa to see if he wanted to go with us."

"And?"

"We're picking him up in a few minutes."

"Great. It'll do him good to get out." Grandpa Steve Holland sometimes got bored when left alone at the home place, where he lived with Cheryl. The house lay a quarter mile down the road, and Robyn maintained her business of raising and training sled dogs there. She went over every day, and Grandpa helped her around the dog yard as much as he was able, but he loved to get out and see folks beyond the family circle. Cheryl did her best to keep him active, and she appreciated Rick and Robyn's efforts to get him out of the house frequently.

Robyn glanced at her watch. "Maybe we'd better remind Rick."

"Yes. We have scheduled patients, starting at ten. If you want to get back before then, you should leave soon."

Robyn leaned toward her. "Before you do that, what do *you* think of Oz?"

"He's terrific, but. . ."

"But what?"

Cheryl grimaced, trying to sort out her feelings. Did they really matter? "He won't last a month."

Robyn's eyebrows shot up. "Why do you say that? So far, he loves it here."

"Yes, but. . . Oh, I don't know. He's always lived in the city, and he's not used to the cold and the long winters."

"Mom, he's originally from upstate New York. They have snow there."

Cheryl shrugged. "I hope I'm wrong."

She hoped so intensely. But she faced the truth. Being around Oz made her giddy, like a sixth grader with a new crush. But no way would this man be a permanent part of her future. He was a suave, educated bachelor from the city, cultured and used to fine things. His wristwatch probably cost more than her car. Before coming to Wasilla, he'd been employed by the San Francisco Zoo, and before that the Philadelphia Zoo.

She was a country girl who'd grown up making do without a lot of things that people like Oz considered necessities. She saved her bread bags to reuse them and tried not to drive into Anchorage more than once a month to save gas. The mother of two grown children, grandmother of a darling baby boy, she valued her family above all else.

Polar opposites.

True, Rick had assured her that Oz was committed to staying at least a year. Which meant that next fall he'd probably pull up stakes again and move to wherever he could get another study grant. Nope, she wasn't going to allow herself to get used to having him around.

The men's voices grew louder as they came out into the waiting room where Cheryl's desk sat.

"Oh, hi, honey." Rick grinned at Robyn. "Ready for our adventure?"

"Yes, and I called Grandpa and he wants to go."

"Great. Let's go get him. Oh, Cheryl. . ." Rick turned toward her. "I'm going to let Oz settle in. He wants to set up his computer and unpack those crates of books that arrived the other day. But he says he'll handle any emergencies that come in while I'm gone, so don't hesitate to call on him. Otherwise, I expect to be back in time for my first appointment at ten, and Oz can shadow me and get a feel for how I work."

"Okay, that sounds fine."

"Bye, Mom. Catch you later." Robyn kissed her cheek and bustled out the door with Rick.

Oz still stood behind her.

Cheryl couldn't see him, but every nerve was aware of his presence. It was almost like standing with her back to a fireplace in a chilly room and letting the warmth of the blaze gradually thaw and then toast her. She turned slowly. "I'll put some coffee on if you'd like."

"Thank you. The jet lag is catching up with me. I must say I'm delighted with the size of my office and the exam rooms."

She smiled. "Rick spent months planning this building and getting advice. He said he intends to work here another forty years, and he wanted to get it right."

"He did a great job." Oz looked around the waiting room and chuckled. "I admit I'm glad you're here. When Rick said he was taking off for a couple of hours, my first thought was, 'Oh no, someone will come in with a cat that needs immediate surgery.' I've spent the last three years working with exotic animals, and the last six months mainly doing research. Haven't treated everyday pets for a long time."

"I'm glad you're here, too. I've done this for over a year now, but I still get nervous when Rick's not here and an injured animal comes in."

"I'm sure you do a great job of calming the owner down and making the patient comfortable."

"I do my best." She took a step toward the hallway. "We have a small kitchen back here. Did Rick show you?"

"Yes, he did."

"I'll start the coffeepot, and you can help yourself whenever you want. We also have a refrigerator for people food, as opposed to the ones for pet food and medicine."

"Wonderful. If I can just remember which is which, I won't have to worry about some husky getting my ham sandwich for lunch."

"Or you getting a salad with a cat food garnish." They both laughed. He was way too easy to talk to. This side of him reminded her of Dan Holland, though he looked nothing like her late husband.

Four years, she thought as she measured the coffee. *Dan has been gone four years.* Could she let go of him enough to let someone new into the deepest part of her heart?

She heard whistling coming from the hallway and paused to listen. Apparently Oz had mastered the twitters and trills of myriad birdcalls and threw them willy-nilly into his rendition of "North to Alaska." She'd have to be careful, or she'd let herself like the new guy too much. But as she walked back to her desk with a bounce in her step, she found herself humming along.

※

Oz set the last of his medical books on a shelf and stood back to catch the effect. With his framed diplomas on one wall and a photo of him with a grizzly bear he'd treated at the San Francisco Zoo hanging over the file cabinets, he was almost done moving into his new office. Most of his personal items had gone to the rental cabin, but he'd bring a few knickknacks here to make it his own space. Maybe the antique dueling pistols he'd bought in Russia last year.

He ran his hand over the surface of the walnut desk. Not too shabby. Rick had spent a lot to make sure his new partner would like working here. Had the time come to settle down for good? Wasilla was a bit provincial, compared to his usual haunts, but Anchorage wasn't far away, if he got a culture craving.

The phone on the desk emitted two quick beeps and he picked up the receiver. "Hello?" Nothing. One button blinked red at him. He pushed it. "Hello?"

"Dr. Thormond, this is Cheryl. A client just called, and her dog had a collision with a motorcycle. She's bringing him in with a fractured leg and possible internal injuries. Since Dr. Baker is out, can you handle it? ETA about ten minutes."

"Uh. . .sure. Take the dog into the first treatment room?"

"That would be Rick's room. Would you like to see Thor in your own treatment space?"

"Certainly. Do we have a file on Thor?"

"Yes, we do. He's a Great Dane, about three years old, and is up to date on his immunizations. I'll bring you his file. Would you like to meet Mrs. Nickerson with me? For a large dog, we usually take the stretcher out to the parking lot."

"Of course."

He hauled in a deep breath as he returned the phone to its cradle. This was going to be a lot different from his work with zoo animals. And so much for Rick being the dog expert. His first patient. Oh well.

Cheryl tapped on the door and entered carrying a manila file folder. "Here you go. He's a healthy dog. Too bad he ran out into the street."

"What happened to the biker?"

"Road burns. He wasn't going very fast, and he was wearing his helmet."

"Good for him."

"Mrs. Nickerson said the young man was quite upset about Thor's injuries, but it wasn't his fault." Cheryl gave him a sympathetic smile. "You're supposed to take over the large animal end of the practice so Rick can concentrate on dogs. Sorry about this."

"Well, it's a *large* dog."

She chuckled. "I'm glad you see the humor. You'll get a good initiation to our stretcher routine."

Oz flipped the file open and scanned Rick's notes on the dog's past visits. "Thor doesn't seem to have had need of anesthesia until now. Let's have some local anesthetic ready, in case we can use that, but we'll probably need to put him out." He gave her the dosage, based on the dog's weight.

While she hurried to set out the medication, syringe, and a set of sterile instruments, Oz scrubbed up and put on gloves. When they were ready, Cheryl wheeled the stretcher from the treatment room into the hallway and out through the waiting room. A beige minivan pulled into the parking lot as they reached the front door.

"That's Allie Nickerson." Cheryl pushed a large button on the wall, and the double doors swung open.

"I'm impressed that Rick sprang for so much technology."

"He wants to give the best animal care in Wasilla. He does, too."

Oz smiled at her fierce loyalty. He pushed the stretcher outside and down the ramp. A woman with long, dark hair in a ponytail leaped from the van and opened the slider door behind the driver's seat.

Cheryl called, "Allie, this is Dr. Thormond, Rick's new partner."

The woman threw him a distracted glance. "Hello."

Cheryl let Oz handle the stretcher and went to the door of the van. "Oh my. I'm sorry this happened."

Oz set the stretcher's brake and stepped up beside Cheryl.

The big dog lay listlessly on the middle seat. His coat was caked with congealing blood on his right side, and his hind leg had obviously sustained a compound fracture.

"Let me lift him, ladies. One quick move will be easiest on him, I think."

They stepped aside.

Oz leaned into the van and rested his weight on his left knee. "Hi, fella. I know you feel lousy. I'm gonna help you." He slid his right arm under the dog's head and neck.

Thor growled, low in his chest.

"Okay, maybe we should give him a tranquilizer first." He backed out of the vehicle.

"I'll get it." Cheryl hurried inside.

For the next forty-five minutes, Oz concentrated on the patient, but he noted that Cheryl never left his side while he examined the Great Dane and operated on his fractured leg. She seemed to know which instrument Oz would need next, and when she hesitated once, he gave her precise instructions. She complied with a minimum of delay. He'd had some qualms about the lack of a well-trained veterinary technician to assist in times like these, but she more than met his expectations. When he'd finished, he peeled off his gloves.

Cheryl gently bathed the blood from the dog's side with warm water. "Shall I give Allie an update?"

"I'll go out and talk to her. Thor's going to need a prolonged recovery, but I'm hoping he'll have full use of that leg back." He pulled off his protective mask and goggles.

"Do you want me to stay with him until you come back?"

He nodded. "Thanks. After I talk to Mrs. Nickerson, we can move Thor to the recovery area and she can see him." He opened the door. Rick hurried down the hallway toward him. Oz called over his shoulder to Cheryl, "Looks like Rick's back."

A flicker of relief tempered the satisfaction that ran through Oz. His first surgery in Alaska was performed on one of Rick's canine patients. He'd just as soon his friend looked the dog over and made sure he hadn't missed anything.

"Hey, Ozzie! Allie just told me you were putting Thor's leg back together. How'd it go?"

"All right. I just finished stitching him up. He's still groggy, but I haven't put the cast on. Thought I'd leave that for you."

Cheryl looked up as they entered. "Hi, Rick."

"How's he doing?"

"Great."

"Internal injuries?" Rick asked.

"Nothing major." Oz put the chart in his hand. "I haven't updated this, but you can see the medications we used."

Rick frowned over it for half a minute. "Looks good. Just what I would have done. We'd better not cast it until that swelling goes down."

"Yeah. Do you want to talk to Mrs. Nickerson?" Oz asked.

"No, you did the surgery. Go ahead." Rick held the door for him.

Oz nodded and headed for the waiting area with a smile. He'd forgotten how great it felt to tell an owner her pet would recover. Treating domestic animals had its perks.

Allie rose, her face pale with strain. "How is he?"

"He's doing well." Oz took a seat and gestured for her to sit down beside him. "Thor came through the surgery fine, but he'll need several weeks of rest. We're going to put a cast on his leg, probably tomorrow. Dr. Baker will take over his care now, and he can advise you on that, but I'm hopeful that Thor will make a complete recovery."

"Thank God." Tears spilled over her eyelids and ran down her cheeks.

Oz reached over to the end table and grabbed a box of tissues. "Here you go. There's nothing to worry about. You'll be able to go in and see Thor in a few minutes, and then we'd like to keep him here at least overnight. When the swelling is down and the cast is on, you'll be able to take him home."

"Thank you so much, Dr. . . ." She blinked at her tears and gazed up at him. "I'm sorry. I've forgotten your name. But thank you."

"Oz Thormond." He smiled and rose. Cheryl stood in the

hall door, watching him. Oz walked over and asked softly, "Is Thor ready to see his owner?"

"Yes, we put him in a low recovery bed. I'll take her in."

"Thanks. And, Cheryl. . ."

She looked up at him with raised eyebrows. Her brown eyes shone with compassion.

"You did great," Oz said. "Thank you for all your help in there. Rick must be very grateful to have an assistant as capable as you are."

Slowly, her smile curved her lips. As she approached Allie, Oz acknowledged that his first day on the job, while challenging, was looking pretty good, and Cheryl's presence played an important part in that.

three

Grandpa Steve came from his bedroom, walking slowly but steadily.

"You all set, Cheryl? We don't want to be late."

She smiled and rose from her armchair. "I'm ready. But you don't have to worry about being late, Dad. It's only next door."

"I know, but I want to meet Rick's new partner. Come on." Steve took his jacket from the closet and pulled it on.

Sometimes living with her father-in-law brought Cheryl a lot of headaches, but for the most part, they got along. He'd helped her and Dan get established when they moved to Alaska, and she found satisfaction in helping him as he grew older. They'd always been good friends, but since Dan's death, they'd drawn even closer. Because of her care, Steve was able to continue living at home.

She took his arm as they went down the front steps. For the hundredth time she wondered if she ought to see about having a ramp built on the house. Right now, he was doing fairly well, but he'd spent some time in the hospital and rehab last winter, and some days he was shaky on his feet.

They made it safely to the car, and Cheryl drove the short distance down the road to Rick and Robyn's house. She parked behind the pickup in their driveway. "Dr. Thormond must have arrived. Robyn's Jeep is right over there."

"Is he going to get a car of his own?" Steve undid the seatbelt and reached for the door latch.

"That's the plan, but Rick told him to take his time and make sure he gets what he wants. He'll probably want a truck or a van."

The door of the spacious log cabin opened, and Robyn skipped down the steps.

"Hey, Grandpa! How are you today?" She kissed him and took his arm as they headed for the house.

"I'm good. I'm always good. Where's this hotshot new vet we've got? I want to see him."

Robyn laughed. "He's inside, and he wants to meet you."

A minute later the two shook hands.

"Oz," said Grandpa. "What kind of name is that? Are you from the Emerald City?"

"No, sir. It's my mother's fault. She named me Oswald, and I've been stuck with the nickname since the cradle."

"Aha." Grandpa looked him up and down. "Well, it doesn't seem to have harmed you any."

"Supper's ready," Robyn said as she led them to the round dining table. "Oz, let's put you there, beside Rick. So how do you like your new digs?"

"It's great. Small, but comfortable. And I think I'll like having the woodstove for backup heat." Oz took a seat between Cheryl and Rick.

Robyn set a pan of lasagna on a trivet and sat down between her husband and Grandpa. Rick reached for her hand.

"Let's ask the blessing." He held out his other hand to Oz.

Grandpa clasped hands with Cheryl and Robyn. "We always do this. Keeps Robby from grabbing a bite while we pray."

Robyn made a face at him.

Cheryl had already grasped Steve's hand. She felt her cheeks heat up as she reached out to Oz and quickly bowed her head. She tried to hold his hand lightly, but not so loosely that he'd think she didn't want to touch him. But too firm a grip might be construed as boldness.

She hardly heard a word of Rick's brief prayer. Instead, she thought about Oz's warm, strong fingers clasping her hand. She still wore her wedding ring. Had he noticed that, and what would he think about it? Since Dan had died, she hadn't seriously thought of beginning a new relationship, but she wasn't totally against it. Of course, a new man entering her personal life would have to meet a high standard. So far Oz had passed all her imaginary tests on professionalism. The jury was still out on adapting to the climate and culture. He'd prayed over lunch the day she picked him up at the airport. How many men would have suggested it when eating out with a stranger?

Rick said, "Amen," and she opened her eyes. Though she was thankful for the meal, the distraction of holding a handsome man's hand had all but eliminated her thoughts of prayer.

Oz released her hand slowly.

She didn't look at him but reached for the salad bowl. Enough of this woolgathering.

"Now, Doc," Grandpa said, fixing Oz with a sober gaze, "have you ever driven a sled team?"

Oz grinned. "That's one of the few things I've never driven. I did ride on a reindeer sled once, but I didn't get to drive."

"Well, you'll have to learn. When you get a day off, you come over, and Robby and I will fix you up with a sled and team."

"Sure, anytime." Robyn smiled at Oz. "When you want a lesson, come on over. I'm sure Grandpa would be happy to boss you around. He does it to me all the time. And it's a good idea for you to get a couple of lessons in case you ever need to drive a sled."

Rick reached for Oz's plate and held it up so Robyn could load it with lasagna. "You know, in winter we use snow machines in the business a lot. More than dog sleds. Sometimes that's the only way to get around to the remote farms and kennels."

Oz nodded. "I did learn to use one of those when I went to Russia. We were doing research on the Siberian ice sheet. Talk about remote! If your machine doesn't run, you've had it."

Grandpa leaned forward, his eyes glittering. "You'll have to tell me more about that. You know, when Danny and I first came up here, we'd never seen a snow machine before, but Danny was keen on getting one right away. He got an old, used Ski-Doo, and he took Cheryl off to see the lake. Well, wouldn't you know it, that thing conked out on him. He was going to walk back on the trail they'd packed and come get her with a dog team, but guess what?"

"Cheryl got the sled running," Oz said.

Grandpa frowned. "No. But that's a pretty good guess. You tell him, Cheryl."

She looked over at Oz and held the salad bowl out to him. This shopworn family tale was far less exciting than Oz's bear tracking in Siberia. "Dan had stopped the machine, and it wouldn't start again. Turns out it was a poor connection to the battery, is all. A family of Tlingit Native Alaskans came along, riding a couple of sleds. They helped us out and got us going again. That's when I decided I needed to know more about engines."

"And she's been our designated mechanic ever since," Grandpa said with a laugh. "Keeps the snow machine and the snow blower and lawnmower running. Not bad when it comes to minor things with her car either. I'm glad she likes it. Someone had to know how to keep the vehicles running, and personally, I'd rather spend time with the dogs."

Cheryl smiled and shook her head. "It's not that I'm so crazy about engines, but someone around here needed to be practical. And those folks who helped us became friends of ours. They still stop in to visit when they come to town." She decided it was time to turn the conversation. Enough about her grease-monkey tendencies. "Oz was telling me that he'll be heading for the North Slope in February."

"Is that right?" Grandpa asked. "I don't guess the mama bears are coming out of their dens yet."

"It's a little early, but we'll get out over the ice pack and tag a lot of adults. And I'm going on a different trip at the end of March or the first part of April. It's usually easiest to locate mothers with new cubs then."

"Maybe you'll be around to help out with the Fire & Ice race here in January and the start of the Iditarod in March," Grandpa said.

"I'm planning on it. I want to jump into the culture here and contribute to the community." Oz smiled across the table at Robyn. "Rick's told me how hard your family works to put on the Fire & Ice. And how hard you're training to run some races yourself. I know he's proud of you."

Robyn shrugged. "I hoped to do the Iditarod this year, but it's going to have to wait. I'm doing a couple of shorter races."

"By next year this time, you'll have your Iditarod team training." Rick winked at his wife then turned back to Oz. "She works harder than anyone else I know. She's wanted to do the Iditarod for a long time, and we really hoped it would be this year. But I trust her judgment. She trains teams for other people, and she'll know when she's got the right dogs."

"We'll all be there to help you and cheer you on," Cheryl said.

"Thanks, Mom." Robyn looked eagerly at their guest. "I'm going to help Rick at the dropped dog station in Anchorage during the Iditarod again this year. That might be something you'd enjoy helping with, Oz."

"What is that?"

"It's where the dogs that are dropped from teams along the trail go to wait for their owners to pick them up after the race."

Rick nodded and handed him a plate of sliced garlic bread. "Sometimes dogs get sick or are injured along the trail, and the musher has to drop them from his team. Somebody has to give them the treatment needed and make sure they're well cared for until the race is over."

"Sounds like an interesting way to support the race," Oz said. "Maybe it will distract me from those long winter nights we'll be getting."

"By then, daylight hours will be lengthening again, but yeah, anything like that helps." Robyn glanced around, and apparently satisfied that all her guests had been served each dish, she began to eat.

Cheryl let the talk flow around her. Dogs, sledding, veterinary patients.

"Back in the old days. . ." Grandpa began, and she stifled a laugh. With a new audience, Steve would probably trot out all his old stories. But that was okay. Oz seemed to have a patient disposition. One more point in his favor. Did his numerous good points outweigh their differences yet? Of course, he'd been to Siberia, and who knew where else. He'd get cabin fever here during the long winter and leave when his research was done.

"Stop it," Cheryl said under her breath.

"Excuse me?" Oz smiled tentatively at her.

"Oh, nothing. I'm sorry."

"She talks to herself," Robyn said.

Cheryl gritted her teeth as her cheeks warmed. "It's a habit I'm trying to break."

four

On Sunday morning Oz attended church with Rick and Robyn. Cold winds blew in from the mountains, promising snow, and for the first time he wore his ultra-warm parka.

He wasn't sure what to expect at the nondenominational church. The structure was much smaller than the one he'd attended in San Francisco, but its members included people of different races and varied ethnic backgrounds. He went with Rick and Robyn to a classroom for Sunday school during the first hour, and they introduced him to the class's leader, Sam Kwon, a young man about Rick's age.

"We're glad to have you here." Sam grinned as he shook Oz's hand. "How do you like Alaska so far?"

"I love it. Had my first mushing lesson yesterday."

"That's terrific," Sam said. "I hope I'll see more of you."

"Is he Korean?" Oz asked Rick as they settled into the third row. "The name sounds like it." He gazed at Sam again, puzzling over the leader's features.

Rick grinned. "His mother's Korean, but his father was born here. Part Russian, part Native Alaskan."

"Aha. Interesting. I hope I'll have a chance to get to know him better."

"No doubt about it," Rick said. "He and his wife, Andi, are good friends of ours, and they're very outgoing."

Oz looked around the class of about thirty people. "Where's Cheryl?"

"Oh, she teaches a primary class. You'll see her after Sunday school, I expect."

Oz couldn't help mentally comparing Cheryl to the women

he was used to in the city. He liked so many things about her:
She took care of her father-in-law, helped out wherever she was
needed at the vet practice, drove a Ski-Doo with the best of the
Alaskans, and taught a children's class. She might lack the polish
of his old acquaintances, but he wasn't sure that was a drawback.
He opened his Bible, determined to listen to Sam and not day-
dream about the lovely, tough, compassionate Cheryl Holland.

After the class, she greeted them warmly at the back of the
church auditorium.

"Good to see you again," Oz said.

"Thank you." She wore a brightly patterned skirt, a knit top,
and a cranberry jacket. Oz had already noted that the church
people didn't waste fuel overheating the building, and she'd
dressed appropriately.

"Mom, where's Grandpa?" Robyn asked.

"He has a cold, and I persuaded him to stay home and rest."

"I hope it's not serious," Oz said.

"I don't think it is, but it's windy and cold today. I didn't want
him getting chilled."

They followed Rick and Robyn down the center aisle.

"How did your class go?" Oz asked.

She smiled at him. "Great. I had eleven children this morning."

He let her enter the pew after Rick and sat on the aisle beside her. Around them, the rows filled quickly. The service was
less formal than his usual fare, but that didn't bother him. He
liked being surrounded by enthusiastic people who put their
hearts into their singing.

Rick and Robyn had both assured him that if he wasn't comfortable at their church they wouldn't be insulted if he chose
another. But he liked this one—the friendliness, the worship-
ful atmosphere, and the plain exposition of God's Word.

Cheryl caught his eye as they stood for the final hymn. She
opened her mouth as if to speak then closed it with a slight
smile.

Did she wonder about his reaction to her home territory? She was too polite to ask. Even though he'd never belonged to a church like this one, he knew the answer to her unspoken query.

He leaned toward her. "Feels like home here."

❧

Four weeks later, Cheryl concluded that Oz had settled into the routine of the office. When she answered the phone, many patients' owners asked for him by name. He'd met dozens of residents and their pets and livestock. Business had picked up so much she was training a friend to man the desk and schedule appointments so she could assist the veterinarians more. Three couples had issued dinner invitations to Oz. He'd told Cheryl with a laugh that if he wasn't careful, his social calendar would be full every weekend.

He seemed to take the late fall weather in stride, too. Eighteen inches of snow had fallen over the valley. Instead of complaining, he'd called a young man Rick had recommended and hired him to plow his driveway. Then he'd set up another dog sledding lesson with Robyn and Grandpa Steve. He'd also taken a snow machine jaunt with a client whose horse he had treated.

Cheryl grudgingly revised her original estimate. Oz showed self-sufficiency she hadn't expected. He'd stayed more than a month. In fact, his first words to her that morning were, "I'm beginning to feel like an Alaskan."

His jaw sported dark stubble that morning. She took note—it only added to his masculine attractions—but she refused to comment. Not for a minute did she believe he'd forgotten or neglected to shave. He was following Rick's example and growing a beard for the winter. The two men had arrived within moments of each other amid falling snow and grabbed shovels from the utility closet to finish clearing the walkway.

It was the first Monday in November. While they shoveled, Cheryl placed a copy of the day's schedule on each man's desk, as she did every day. Today Oz's entire morning was scheduled with barn calls. Rick would see patients in the office while Oz traveled around to vaccinate livestock and check on ill and injured horses and cattle. That was all right. She'd be able to concentrate better and get more done while he was out of the office. In spite of her good intentions, she found herself keeping track of him when he was in the building and listening for his voice. Not today. She'd continue training Angela to man the front desk and catch up on her filing.

About ten o'clock, Angela fielded a call and turned to Cheryl for help. "It's Hal Drake. He wants a doctor to come to his ranch."

Drake was a regular client with a large herd of beef cattle. "Put him through to Rick," Cheryl said. They didn't give out the doctors' cell phone numbers unless it was urgent.

A woman and her twelve-year-old daughter came in with their cat in a plastic cage.

"Have a seat," Cheryl told them with a smile. "Dr. Baker will be right with you." She walked down the hallway to inform Rick that his next patient had arrived.

When she looked into his office, he was hanging up his phone. "Guess I'd better call Ozzy on his cell. Sounds like we have a big problem out at the Drakes'."

⁂

"I've done what I can for now," Oz said, examining an Arabian horse's front leg. "Her pastern's swollen, and it seems tender. Keep doing the cold packs. I'll come by tomorrow, and we'll see if it looks any better."

"All right, thanks." The owner was a young woman whose family owned four saddle horses. The mare had stumbled and wrenched her pastern earlier that morning, and Cheryl had added the stop to his list of calls.

He set the mare's hoof gently on the floor and straightened his back. "Just keep her in the barn tonight and let her rest."

"Thanks. I will."

As Oz headed for the pickup he'd bought the week before, the sun was just rising, although it was after ten o'clock. His phone rang, and he fumbled in the pocket of his jacket for it.

"Oz, it's Rick. We have another barn call for you, and this one sounds serious. A beef rancher who's a regular client has one cow dead and several others symptomatic with an undiagnosed illness. I'll head out there as soon as I finish with the patient I'm treating now, but we may both need to be there."

"Sure. How do I get there? I'm at the Lilleys' place now."

"Why don't you swing by and pick up Cheryl? She's a little skittish around cattle, but she's helped me once or twice. She's great at keeping the records for you and running back and forth to the truck."

"Okay, if you're sure. I'll come back right now."

"Yeah, I think that's best. From Mr. Drake's description, we might need an extra pair of hands. Angela's here, and she can cover the desk while we're out."

On his short drive to the animal hospital, Oz found himself anticipating working closely with Cheryl. She'd helped him a few times with animals he'd treated at the office. She stayed calm and seemed to know what to do before he asked. Rick had chosen well when he picked his office manager.

When he reached the practice, Cheryl jogged down the steps carrying a large tote bag and climbed into his truck. "Hi. Turn left out of the parking lot. It's four or five miles."

Oz took the pickup out onto the road, a little surprised at her terse directions. "Thanks for coming."

"I hope I can be of some help. I can record tag numbers and dosages for you. Just don't ask me to herd cows."

He smiled. Her mouth was set in a grim line, and he guessed Rick had understated her feelings toward cattle.

❧

How did I get into this? Cheryl bounced along with Oz in the truck, up the long farm lane. If the farmer's situation hadn't sounded so urgent, she'd have said no. She was surprised Rick had offered her services. Since when did he think she was an expert at assisting with treating sick cattle? She'd helped him once and nearly lost a finger to an inquisitive cow. Instead of greeting patients in the comfortable office, she'd soon be standing in a barnyard in the ten-degree wind.

"I shouldn't have agreed so quickly," she muttered.

"Did you say something?" Oz looked over and smiled at her.

"No, but I'm really not on very good terms with cows. And these belong to the big, shaggy variety."

"That's right. Scottish Highlands, Rick said. They have very long hair."

"And very big horns."

He chuckled. "They're quite docile, I understand. I've never been close to one myself."

She gulped. At least she had thermal mittens and hat, besides her warm parka and high boots.

"If it makes you feel better, the owner usually helps if I need someone to hold an animal still," Oz said. "If you can keep handing me instruments and filling in the records, we'll do fine."

Even with his vivid blue eyes holding her gaze for a moment, Cheryl couldn't quite believe him. She loved animals, but cattle at close range put her on edge. She should have simply refused to go. On the other hand, if she could hold it together, her presence would save him time and headaches. She determined to make this trip worthwhile if it killed her. Which wasn't out of the realm of possibility, given those wicked horns on the beasts. She let out a long sigh.

"Not thrilled about this, are you?" Oz asked. "Sorry."

"Oh, please, it's not the company. Yet."

He laughed. "I know, I know. It's them." He nodded toward the fence that ran alongside the lane.

They'd approached the farm buildings, and several dozen

cattle awaited them, milling about in a large holding pen. One especially large and hairy specimen fixed them with a doleful gaze and lowed.

"Chin up," Cheryl told herself. "You can do this."

"Yes, you can." Oz brought the truck to a halt before the barn and smiled over at her.

"Oh. Sorry. I didn't mean to say it out loud."

"It's okay. If you need a pep talk while we're working, just say so, and I'll be happy to give you one."

"Okay, now I feel silly. It's the horns, mostly. And the hooves. Cows' hooves can be very sharp, you know."

"Oh yes." He grinned as he opened his door and climbed out of the truck.

"Well, we're here to save sick animals. I'll try to focus on that." She didn't wait for him to come and open her door. This wasn't a social outing after all. It was work. She jumped down and pulled her clipboard from her tote bag.

She wondered, not for the first time, if her son-in-law was trying his hand at matchmaking. She already suspected Grandpa Steve of that when he'd tried to persuade her to give Oz his dog sledding lessons. She'd quickly quashed that idea, pointing out that of all the family she was the least skilled in mushing, though she was competent. Oz would be much better off with Robyn as instructor.

When Rick had told her Oz needed her to guide him to the Drakes' ranch, she'd watched him for a moment, looking for anything that would betray a smugness or self-satisfaction. She couldn't detect any insincerity. He'd had the decency to thank her and say, "You don't mind, do you? I suppose I should have asked you before mentioning it to Ozzy."

And she'd said, "No, it's all right." So she couldn't blame Rick that she was now walking to the fence where Hal Drake, his wife, and three ranch employees stood bleakly waiting for Oz's opinion. She refused to consider the possibility that she had accepted the challenge in order to be near Oz. He had nothing to do with it. She was here for the Drakes and their animals. And she'd do a good job. Period.

Oz entered the pasture and walked over to the corner, where the others stood near a dead Scottish Highland cow.

Cheryl stayed outside the fence, a few feet away. That was close enough, in her book.

five

"It looks like red nose." Drake raised his hands helplessly. "Can't see how that could be. We vaccinated every animal last spring."

"I'm going to take some lab samples, and we'll find out for sure," Oz told him. "Meanwhile, you need to isolate any that look sick."

He walked over to the fence. "Cheryl, I'm going to get my instrument bag. Can you grab a box of latex gloves out of the back, please? And I'll need supplies to take some fluid samples."

When they reached the truck, she began gathering what he needed. Efficient, as always. He called Rick's cell phone, and his friend answered on the first ring.

"Hey, buddy. Looks like IBR, but they vaccinated. Have you got anything that will help?"

"We've got some vaccine on hand, but not enough. If that's what it is, we'll need more."

"Right. I think I'd better take samples from the dead animal and bring it back to look at under the microscope."

"Do you want me to run it in the lab, while you examine the other sick cattle?"

"Might be a good idea. Why don't you stay there and treat any patients who come in? Set up the scope, and I'll send Cheryl back with some samples. You can call me as soon as you're sure what we've got."

"Okay," Rick said. "That's probably the most efficient way to do it."

"Until I know for sure what we're dealing with. . ." He signed off.

Cheryl closed the rear window on the truck cap. "I think I've got everything you need."

"Did you hear what I told Rick?"

"Yes. I'd be happy to take the blood samples back to the office."

"Thanks. I think that's best."

He got his bag from the front of the truck and they walked back to the fence. He went through the gate, and she handed him a pair of gloves over the top. Drake and his helpers had gone to check on the rest of the herd and weed out any showing symptoms. Oz put on his surgical gloves and began taking samples from the dead cow, thinking of other diseases that could cause symptoms similar to those of IBR.

Cheryl put the identifying labels on the vials.

"I'll get a couple more samples from cattle that are showing symptoms."

Her brow furrowed, and the corners of her eyes drew down. "Doesn't look good, does it?"

"Nope."

A few minutes later, he laid the last vials in the cooler and shut the lid securely. "Have Rick call me, okay?"

"Sure."

"And pray. They've got three hundred cattle here. If this is a contagious disease, it could devastate them."

Cheryl nodded soberly. "We'll let you know as soon as we can. And I'll be praying every minute."

⋆

Cheryl kept busy doing online research while Rick made slides and examined them. The disease they suspected was a nasty one. She kept thinking about how well Oz had handled the situation. She'd enjoyed the chance to watch him in action. He worked quickly and confidently and moved with ease among the cattle. He'd seemed at home on the ranch, in spite of his metropolitan background. She'd misjudged him. Oz could adapt to any situation and enjoy it to the hilt.

After fifteen minutes, she went to the door of the small laboratory near the back of the building.

Rick was still hunched over the microscope. He pulled away from the eyepiece and jotted something in his notebook.

"Got a diagnosis?" she asked.

"Yes. It's IBR all right. Drake must have gotten a bad batch of vaccine." He looked over his shoulder at her. "Guess I'd better call Ozzy." He stood and stretched. "Pull all the vaccine we've got, and I'll order more."

She went to the refrigerator and took out a case of glass vials.

"Hey, Oz," Rick said behind her. "You were right on the money. Can you ask Mr. Drake what drug company he got his vaccine from last spring?" He paused, pacing back and forth in the small room while Cheryl checked for more bottles of the medicine. "McPhail Pharmaceuticals? Does he have the paperwork with the batch number? Great." He leaned over the desk and jotted more notes.

In Cheryl's Internet research, she'd discovered that infectious bovine rhinotracheitis was a virus that caused respiratory infections in cattle. If the Drakes hadn't separated the ill cattle from the healthy ones soon enough, the entire herd could've been affected. Besides breathing difficulties, it could lead to numerous problems including eye infections, spontaneous abortions in cows, and even the brain infection encephalitis.

"Yeah, we'll have to notify the company and see if anyone else has had trouble with that batch of vaccine." Rick ended his phone call and came to look over Cheryl's shoulder. "That's all we've got?"

"Yes. Enough for a hundred and forty doses."

"Well, we'll have to inoculate the entire herd. It won't cure them, but it will keep any that aren't infected from getting the disease. I'd better call some other vets and see if anyone has more vaccine we can borrow."

"Angela and I'll make the calls. You need to get to the Drake ranch with what we've got."

"You sure?"

"Yes. Any vet who's got some will be happy to donate it and will probably come and help you administer it. If I can't find enough in Wasilla, I'll call Anchorage."

"Great. And if the vets don't have it on hand, try some of the other farmers." Rick put his arm around her and gave her shoulders a squeeze. "I knew I was getting a gem when I hired you."

Cheryl smiled at him. "Thanks."

She immediately sat down to phone other veterinary practices in the Wasilla-Palmer area. Within an hour, she and Angela had obtained promises of 180 more doses of the needed vaccine from two local veterinarians. Before sending them to the Drake ranch with the medicine, she had them confirm that their vaccine was not from the same company as that which Drake had used earlier.

She phoned Rick with the news that the other vets had come through for them. "Dr. Kane and a tech from Dr. Rodriquez's office are on the way."

"Terrific."

"How's it going?" she asked. "Can I come help you, or would I just be in the way?"

"Come ahead, if you want to get filthy. I've got forty more doses of vaccine from our batch to administer. Ozzy's treating the six affected animals they've isolated. It's not pretty, but you could mix up disinfectant for him and fetch and carry between the truck and the barn."

Cheryl hurried to gather a few items and pull on her warm outerwear. This time she felt no reservations about joining Rick and Oz at the ranch, though it meant spending a chilly November afternoon waiting on smelly, sick cattle. Was her love of animals expanding to include bovines, or was it the satisfaction she found in helping the veterinarians in the field? She even reflected that it might, after all, have something to do with a certain vet who was out there treating the cattle without regard to his own discomfort. She wouldn't analyze that too deeply.

She drove to the takeout window at a fast-food place on the way and loaded up on coffee and sandwiches. Driving out of town, she marveled at the colors the late November sun painted on the snowy mountains. They were down to about four hours of sunlight each day now, and she loved getting out of the office during the brightest hours.

When she pulled in at the ranch, she could see Rick and Dr. Hilda Kane in the middle of a herd of cattle, confined in a small pen near the barn.

"Hey! How's it going?" she called.

"Not bad," Rick said. "Only about fifty more to go."

"I've got hot coffee and burgers, if you can take a break."

"Don't say that in front of these beef cows," Dr. Kane said with a laugh. "But that sounds good."

"We'll be there in a sec," Rick told Cheryl. "Ozzy's in the barn. He'd probably love to have some black coffee about now."

Cheryl took two of the covered cardboard cups from the holder and carried them into the barn. She found Oz with Mr. Drake, examining a yearling steer. "Hot coffee," she said brightly.

"Oh, bless you, Cheryl." Oz straightened and stripped off one latex glove. "Black?"

"As the mud on your nose. Or is that manure?"

He wiped his nose with his sleeve and reached for the coffee.

Cheryl laughed. "There you go. Would you like some, Mr. Drake?"

"No thanks. My wife's been out twice to tell me my dinner's getting cold."

"Maybe you should go eat," Oz said.

"Maybe I will. You must be hungry, too, Doc."

"I've got sandwiches for him and the others in my car," Cheryl said.

Drake nodded. "All right then, I'll get a bite. You think we're gonna beat this, though, don't you, Doc?"

"I do. We're doing everything we can. When we're done re-vaccinating, it will be up to you to watch for more affected animals and get them out of the herd as quickly as you can."

"Reckon the boys and I can do that."

"And you can't slaughter any animals for sixty days. Don't forget."

"Don't worry, I won't." Drake headed for the house.

Oz leaned against the wall and sighed. "Coffee never tasted so good. Thanks."

Cheryl smiled up at him. "Do you really think you've stopped the infection?"

"Can't say for sure. Rick's been on the lookout for more symptomatic cattle while he inoculates the herd. We haven't found any new cases for the last hour. But only time will tell. This thing's nasty. It can resurface weeks, months, or even years later." He raised his coffee cup again to drink. Fine lines showed at the corners of his eyes and mouth.

"Tired?" she asked.

"Yeah, and the day's only half over." He shook his head. "Guess my age is catching up to me."

"I've got burgers in the car. They should still be warm."

"Oh, you said the magic word."

They walked outside together. Rick, Dr. Kane, and a young man Cheryl didn't know were washing up in a bucket of water and disinfectant on the tailgate of Rick's pickup.

"Hey, Cheryl," Rick called. "I saw that you'd brought enough lunch for an army, so I invited Hilda and Jerry to join us."

"That was my plan." Cheryl handed out wrapped sandwiches. "Hope everybody likes coffee. I've got extra cream and sugar here if anyone wants it."

"Thanks," said Jerry. "I was just heading out on my lunch hour when Dr. Rodriquez asked if I could come here and bring you some extra vaccine."

"Let's go in the barn," Oz said. "It's quite warm in there."

They found seats inside on hay bales. The temperature felt almost balmy. The three vets and Jerry launched into a discussion of the cattle's prognosis as they ate.

Cheryl sat back and listened, sipping her coffee. She looked up at one point.

Oz winked at her.

Her heart lurched. "Very blue eyes," she whispered, so low that no one could hear.

Even so, his eyebrows shot up, and those blue orbs seemed to twinkle.

On the way home, she somehow wound up riding with Oz again. She tried to tell herself that Rick had arranged it, but she and Oz hadn't objected.

Her admiration for "the new guy" had grown today, but her own self-confidence had plunged. The stark differences between her and the man she'd come to admire nagged her.

She hadn't left Alaska for more than twenty years, and she wasn't sure she ever wanted to. But Oz was a world traveler. Educated. Her own high school diploma and one year of college hadn't bothered her before. She'd left school to marry Dan, and when he'd gotten the offer for the Alaska job, they'd gladly left behind all they knew.

But now her low-key, small-town life seemed boring and inadequate compared to Oz's exciting international adventures. She'd loved her family, raised her children, and helped in the family business. A big night out for her was a trip to the huge bookstore in Anchorage. How could someone like Oz find her interesting?

Admitting that she wanted him to find her interesting sobered her.

The sun shone on the glittering landscape as they drove back toward the office. The wind picked up handfuls of loose snow and swirled them across the road to pile up in drifts against the ridges left behind by the snowplow.

"You were a lot of help," Oz said.

"Thanks. You were terrific. I could almost see how you do the polar bear research. I guess it's not that much different from what you did with those cattle today."

"There are some parallels. But you can't just walk up to a bear and stick it with a needle the way you can a steer."

They rode in silence for a few minutes until her curiosity got the better of her. "How do you get close to the polar bears?"

"Usually we fly over and tranquilize them from the air."

"Is that what you'll do when you go to Barrow?"

He nodded. "Yes. In February, if we get a good window on weather, I'll go up for a couple of weeks, and we'll use a helicopter to get out on the edge of the ice sheet. When we see a bear, we'll tranquilize it. Then we'll land and tag it, take samples, and put a radio collar on it. But in the spring, when we concentrate on the denning area, we'll do things differently."

"You told me you want to tag cubs."

"Right. I hope to go when the mamas and babies first come out of their dens. That's my late March trip. I want to tag a significant number of cubs if I can."

"When you put a radio collar on a bear, how long do you follow it?"

"Over its lifetime, if we can. Polar bears can live more than twenty years. But we can't put collars on the little ones. They grow too fast, and the collar would choke one before we could get back and change it. If we make it too loose, the cub slips it off. So we usually collar the mother."

That made sense. "How long do the cubs stay with her?"

"More than two years. Then mama drives them away and starts a new family." Oz pulled into the parking lot.

Cheryl reached for her clipboard and gloves. "I'll call the clients you didn't get around to today and explain."

"Thanks. I'll try to see them all tomorrow." Oz pulled the keys from the ignition. "I've decided I need to get my pilot's license. Is there a flight school in Wasilla?"

Cheryl froze and stared at him. "Do you have to?"

"No, I don't suppose it's really necessary, but it seems the best way to get around this state. I hear Alaska has more licensed pilots per capita than any other state."

"That's true. And fewer miles of roads." She gave a little cough, but the heaviness in her chest didn't budge. Flying was safe, everyone said. Safer than driving a car on Alaska's sorely limited highway system. But the fact that she'd lost Dan in a small plane crash outweighed all the statistics anyone could throw at her. "I. . .I don't know." She avoided his piercing gaze.

"Well, it's just something I thought might come in handy." Oz kept his tone light and opened his door.

Cheryl jumped out quickly and headed for the office. If Oz had wanted to squelch the possibility of a romance, he'd done it effectively. Saving hundreds of woolly cattle and chasing polar bears with a dart gun she could live with. But she would not lose another man she loved in a plane crash.

six

Several weeks later, Oz returned to the office after a long day on the road.

"Hello!" Cheryl turned from the bank of filing cabinets and smiled at him. "Does it feel like the shortest day of the year?"

"Ha! If you go by how tired I am, it's more like the longest."

Twilight had covered the valley three hours ago, and he'd made his last four barn calls in the dark.

"You should go home and rest."

"I will, after I restock my supplies and file my paperwork. Is Rick still here?"

"Yes. Our last patient left about ten minutes ago. Maybe he's writing reports."

Oz ambled down the hall and rapped smartly on the door of Rick's office. "You in there, Richard?"

"Yeah, come on in."

Oz opened the door. Rick was leaning over his desk, with several catalogs spread out on its surface.

"What's up?" Oz asked.

"Cheryl was going to re-order some supplies, and I realized our business has increased dramatically this fall. I'm trying to predict what we'll need over the next quarter. And I'm looking at the prices on those large-animal operating tables, too."

"It would be an extravagance," Oz said. "I think those things are solid gold."

"We'd have the only one in Alaska. . . ." Rick stared off out the window, and his eyes took on a dreamy glaze.

"Quit that." Oz sat down on the corner of his desk. "I can operate on cows and horses where they're lying. Always have.

We don't need to lay out umpteen thousand dollars for fancy equipment."

"It would make your job easier."

Oz shrugged. "I do 90 percent of my work in the field. You know that. We don't get racehorses that need tendon surgery in here."

"True." Rick closed one of the catalogs and shoved it aside. "Just dreaming."

"Well, if you're serious about making me a full partner, I'll put it to you straight. Don't spend all our profits on equipment we don't need."

Rick arched his eyebrows. "Of course I want you to be a full partner. Does this mean you've reached a decision? You'll stay?"

Oz ran a hand through his hair. "I don't think I've ever worked so hard in my life as I have here. But I love it. And the people I work with—well, you and Cheryl are the best. I mean that. And so long as you're willing to let me take a few weeks off two or three times a year for research—in addition to my vacation time, of course—then, yes. I can't think of anything I'd like more."

Rick grinned. "Terrific. We feel the same about you, Ozzy. So, can I announce this happy merger at Christmas dinner?"

Oz smiled and lifted a shoulder. "Sure. Why not?"

"We'll make it official after New Year's, if that's okay." Rick closed the rest of the catalogs and stood. "I'll ask the lawyer to draw up an agreement with the terms we discussed."

"Great. Hey, Rick, there's something else I'd like to talk to you about."

"Yeah? What?"

"You know the research trip I'm taking in the spring?"

"Yeah, that's coming right up, isn't it?"

"Well, for the first one, we'll do most of our spotting from a helicopter. But on the second trip—late March—I'll be in a totally different situation. I'm going with several other scientists. We'll be working on different projects for a couple of weeks. Most of the others are geologists. I'm the only biologist on that jaunt, and I'm supposed to bring an assistant to help with my research."

"Ozzy, I'd love to go, but I don't think we can both leave the practice for two weeks."

Oz sat up straighter. "Sorry. I wasn't actually thinking of you."

"Oh. Bummer." Rick laughed. "What were you going to say then?"

"I was thinking..." Oz frowned at him. "Is this where I should say, 'Oh, come on, I really need you,' and beg you to go?"

"No, I'm serious. I can't do it. It will be right after the Iditarod, and it's a busy time of year for us...lots of animal babies being born."

"Right." Oz hesitated, but there was only one way to get Rick's candid opinion. "I was thinking of asking Cheryl."

Rick sat back down, never taking his eyes from Oz's face. "You're serious."

"Well, sure. I need someone to help me in the field and with the record-keeping and to spot for me. They don't like you to go out alone in such a remote location. Cheryl's been terrific with the domestic animals. I can tell she's worked hard to overcome her"—he paused and groped for a word—"I wouldn't call it fear, but her apprehension toward cattle."

Rick laughed. "She has gotten over a lot of her uneasiness in working with large animals. She still respects them, but she's not afraid to get into a corral with a dozen cows anymore. I credit you with that—hauling her around on so many barn calls."

"She's terrific. I couldn't do without her on a lot of cases." Oz waited, eyeing him thoughtfully.

Rick pulled in a deep breath. "Sure. I guess it's okay. Angela's doing quite well on the desk." He glanced up at Oz. "That's another thing Cheryl's been good at—training her substitute receptionist."

"Yeah, she's good at a lot of things." When he looked back at Rick, Oz couldn't help noticing that his smile reached from ear to ear. "What?"

"Nothing. Need any advice on what to get her for Christmas?"

"Oh man! I meant to order something a couple of weeks ago and I forgot. What do you think I should get her? I've got something on the way for you and Robyn, but. . ."

"Chocolate's good." Rick shoved up out of his chair. "And speaking of my beautiful wife, I'm heading home. How about you?"

"I'm going to stay a little while and do some paperwork. But maybe I'd better think about going to Anchorage tomorrow night and doing some shopping."

"Candy. . .books. . .flowers. . ."

Oz scowled at him. "Flowers? Are you nuts? That's not a Christmas gift. What are you getting her?"

"Robyn picked out a bracelet and a quiviet shawl."

"Ah. And for Robyn?"

"A new stud dog for her breeding kennel."

"Oh. Guess that's not something Cheryl would want."

Rick laughed. "I don't think so. A little pricey for a coworker, too. But if you're serious about taking her to the North Slope, you might consider a snowsuit. I'm not sure if she has a good one. I can ask Robyn if you like."

Oz stood and picked up his clipboard. "Maybe I should see if she's interested in going first."

"Yeah. Whatever." Rick nodded and strode toward the door. "See you in the a.m."

Oz went to his office, thinking over the conversation. Chocolate? Cheryl rarely ate sweets, as far as he knew. Books? Maybe a cookbook or something on gardening. He'd learned she liked those activities.

He could hear her moving about in the waiting room. Was she really the right person to take along on the research trip, or was his attraction to her coloring his decision? Maybe he should ask for a university student or another veterinarian— someone with more scientific training.

A rustle at the doorway made him turn. She stood there smiling, wearing her rose-colored sweater and black slacks. Her vibrant expression, as usual, made him feel as though he belonged here.

Would he regret coming to a place where he felt accepted as part of the family? Forming a closer bond with Rick, whom he loved like a younger brother? Caring about Cheryl and Robyn and Grandpa as though they belonged to him, too?

"I'm going home, Oz. Can you lock up when you leave?"

"Sure."

"Is there anything I can get you before I go?"

"No, but. . ."

She waited, her eyebrows arched and an expectancy lighting her expression.

"Uh. . .I was wondering." He swallowed hard. Maybe he'd better spend some more time with her and get a better feel for her commitment to the job. He didn't want to ask her now and regret it later. After all, he'd only known her for a couple of months.

"Yes?"

What sort of outing could they enjoy together? He stood and walked toward her. "Do you ski?"

"Not much. I've been cross-country skiing several times, but if you mean the alpine kind, it's not my forte."

"Ah." Chuck that idea. She probably didn't want to hear about his past weekends at Aspen and Sun Valley anyway. "Well, I've had several mushing lessons, and I wondered if you'd like to go sledding with me Saturday. Robyn said she'd loan me a team anytime, and I'm sure she'd do the same for her mother."

Cheryl sobered and looked away. He thought for a moment she'd refuse. When she turned her gaze back to him, her smile had changed. It was smaller and softer now. Almost shy, like that first day when she'd had lunch with him on the way here from the airport. "That sounds like a lot of fun."

He looked down at her for a long moment. He'd asked her for a date. An employee. His best friend and almost-partner's mother-in-law. Was he nuts? Gazing into her shimmery brown eyes, he felt very sane. "Great. I'll fix it with Robyn."

"Of course that's Christmas Eve, but if we go early. . ."

"Yes. We'll want to take advantage of the daylight, such as it is." He flicked an involuntary gaze toward the window. Full darkness cloaked the gorgeous view of the mountains.

She nodded, her smile back to the bigger one she greeted patients with. "All right then. Thanks for asking me, and I'll see you tomorrow."

She left, and he let out a long, slow breath. Was this what he wanted? Somehow he felt that Rick and Robyn wouldn't object. In fact, Rick would probably jump for joy when he heard the news. But what if Oz decided after one date that he didn't want to pursue a deeper relationship with Cheryl? Would the entire Holland family hate him? The thought of disappointing Cheryl troubled him.

And yet. . .what if it worked? What if this was God's will in bringing him here? Oz felt a little guilty. He hadn't prayed before he'd asked her. Maybe this was all a mistake.

He sat down in his desk chair with a thud. He admitted he was attracted to Cheryl. What was not to like? But it might be a mistake to get romantic too soon. Or to let her think of romance. Better not give her anything personal for Christmas. Books, like Rick had suggested. That was the ticket. And he'd keep it on a strictly friendly basis Saturday.

Now that he'd asked her out, would it be difficult to separate business and pleasure with Cheryl? If he asked her to go on the polar bear research trip, that had to be business only. But that was three months away. What if they'd decided by then that they didn't like each other all that much?

He leaned back and put his feet up on the desk, careful to set his heels on the blotter, not the shiny walnut surface. Asking Cheryl out felt right, the way driving a truck and burning wood at his cabin felt right. He'd lived under primitive circumstances before, but only for a couple of weeks at a time. He liked Alaska, and the decision to stay and go partners with Rick was another thing that felt right.

He couldn't imagine winding up in an uncomfortable situation. But it could happen if he and Cheryl started something and then one of them backed off. They could end up miserable and having to work together every day. He hated that idea. But then, he'd never seriously considered getting deeply involved with a woman again. Maybe he should follow his original plan and keep it friends only. Things hadn't escalated too far for that.

Still, he hadn't felt this content since before Jo died, more than ten years ago. Even then, he'd been unhappy in his career. He was ready to settle down again, as incredible as that may seem. His restlessness and eagerness to move on to the next project had waned, and he wanted to stay here. Yes, he still got excited when he thought about his research, but he'd also have Wasilla to come home to when it was done. That thought sent a warm glow all through him. He'd found home.

Lord, give me wisdom where Cheryl is concerned, along with the business and everything else in my life.

There. If he kept that attitude foremost in his mind, he wouldn't let his emotions get out of hand. He lowered his feet to the floor and opened the folder of notes he'd made at his barn calls.

seven

Driving a team of four huskies full of energy, Cheryl followed Oz's sled along the trail. She'd driven this route dozens of times in the past. She used to exercise teams regularly when Dan was alive, but she rarely went sledding anymore. Robyn and Grandpa Steve had taken over the kennel after Dan died, and she'd divided her time between her outside jobs and maintaining the home.

It felt good to be out in the crisp air. The temperature had climbed to thirty degrees, and with the sun shining down the valley, it felt almost warm. She lowered the zipper on the front of her parka halfway to let some air in.

Ahead of her, Oz approached a bend in the trail on the hillside above Rick and Robyn's log home. When they rounded the curve, they'd be able to look down on the veterinary clinic.

"Gee," Oz called to his dogs.

Cheryl didn't pay attention at first, but when he yelled, "Gee!" louder and a bit perturbed, she snapped her gaze forward.

"I mean *haw*," Oz called. "Haw! Oh, rats!"

The dogs had swerved off the trail to the right, and the sled bounced up over a ridge of snow. Oz flew off the back, his arms flailing, and landed in eighteen inches of powder. The dog team continued on, curving around downhill, toward the clinic.

If the dogs hadn't been loose, Cheryl would have stopped to laugh and pull Oz out of the snow. Instead, she steered her own team after his, calling, "Whoooooa, Tumble! Whoa, boy!"

She trailed his team for a hundred yards, calling all the time to the leaders, until Tumble, Robyn's prize breeding male, usually very savvy on the trail, slowed to a walk then stopped. The rest of the team followed his example.

"Stay, Tumble," Cheryl called as her own team pulled alongside them. Tumble stood obediently. Cheryl set the snow hook on her own sled then plodded through the loose fluff to Oz's rig and took his hook from where it hung below the handlebar. She pushed it into the snow then stepped on it firmly with one foot. "Hike."

The two leaders—Tumble and his harness mate, Keet—stepped forward a little, and the other dogs followed, pulling the towline taut. "Good boy," Cheryl called. "Line out."

Tumble lay down in the snow, and the rest of the team copied him.

"What can I say? I don't know my right from my left."

She turned around.

Oz slogged through the snow toward her. Tufts of snow clung to his hat and beard. His sheepish smile warmed her.

"More likely you don't know your gee from your haw. I can help you with that."

"Oh? You mean there's hope for me?"

"Definitely. We did it for Robyn when she was about five years old, and it worked like a charm."

"What's that?"

"I took a permanent marker and wrote a *G* on the back of her right glove and an *H* on the left one. On each side of her handlebar, too. I don't think she ever made that mistake again."

"I hate to admit it, but I think I need it until my brain adjusts to the new terminology."

She nodded, trying to keep her expression neutral, but a laugh burbled up from deep inside her. She tried to swallow it, but she couldn't. It burst out as a whoop. "You sure did look funny, flying off into the snow."

Oz grinned. "I'm glad I provided so much entertainment. And thanks for stopping my team."

"You're welcome. They probably would have just gone home, but you never know. They might have run out into the road, looking for a shortcut."

He eyed the placid dogs thoughtfully. "It still seems like I ought to have reins or something."

"Nope. Just your voice. That and the dogs' training are all you've got to control them with."

"Gives me a new appreciation for the people who trained them. . .and for the dogs. Especially the dogs."

"They're awesome. Very intelligent. My advice is to give each a kibble, and we'll head for home. How does hot chocolate sound?"

"Great, if you have time."

"Sure. The kids aren't coming over until suppertime. I know the sun's going down, but we've got a couple of hours. Let's go put these mutts away and sit by the fireplace for a while."

The glint in his blue eyes set her stomach fluttering. She wouldn't have admitted it to anyone, but for two days she'd been thinking about what would happen after their sled run. Oz and a mug of cocoa in front of a snapping log fire. Of course, Grandpa would be there, too. Elderly in-laws were almost as good at killing romance as children. But Oz had opted to spend the entire day with her. At suppertime, Rick and Robyn would join them, and they'd celebrate Christmas together. Oz spending the holiday with her and the family meant something—how much, Cheryl wasn't sure yet.

"You ready?" she asked, ignoring how cute Oz looked with little icicles in his dark beard.

"I think so." He went to the back of his sled and stood with one foot on the brake and the other on the runner nearest his snow hook.

Cheryl stood on her sled's brake and leaned down to pull her hook from the snow. They wended homeward through the sparse woods with her team leading. She stopped them a quarter mile from the dog yard and pointed. Oz's team halted behind hers. They stood for a moment, gazing out over the valley as the rays of the sun hit the distant mountain peaks, scattering scarlet, orange, and purple shadows across the summits.

Cheryl hauled in a deep breath and zipped up her parka. *Thank You, Lord. That is one gorgeous sunset.* She turned forward and called, "Hike!" Her leaders bounded forward, toward home.

❦

As the dog teams trotted into their home yard, Robyn came from the small barn. Darby Zale, the teenager who helped her with kennel chores, watched them from inside the puppy pen.

"Whoa," Oz called, and this time his dogs obliged him by stopping neatly, with the leaders' noses a couple of yards behind Cheryl's sled runners.

"How was your run?" Robyn asked, approaching his team.

"Great." Oz took care to set the snow hook correctly before he stepped off the back of the sled.

"We had a fantastic view of the sunset," Cheryl said.

Oz walked forward to unhook the leaders. Robyn was already unclipping Tumble, and Darby helped Cheryl with her team.

"You don't have to do that, Robyn," he said. "Your mom and I had all the fun. We can put away our dogs and equipment."

"I don't mind."

He wondered if she was evaluating the dogs to see if he'd run them too hard. He glanced over at Cheryl. She grinned at him as she walked with one of her dogs toward the pen where Robyn housed all her grown female dogs. Cheryl could have gotten some laughs by telling how he'd messed up his commands and tumbled into the snow, but she didn't. He appreciated that. He'd have laughed it off if she did tell the story, but somehow it made him like her more that she protected his fragile male ego. Maybe after a day or two, he'd tell the tale himself, but right now his elbow still smarted from the landing, and he'd rather choose the moment when the memory wasn't so fresh. He passed Robyn on his way into the male dogs' pen with Keet.

"Hey, Mom," she called, "after Darby and I feed the dogs, I'm going to take Grandpa over to our house for a little while."

Cheryl paused after hitching the gate to the other pen. "You don't need to do that."

Oz noted her dismay. Was she upset that Robyn was attempting to leave them alone for a while?

"I want to show him something. We won't be gone long." Robyn looked at her watch. "In fact, by the time we feed the dogs, I'll only have about an hour before Rick and I are due here for supper and the Christmas tree."

"Well, get to it then," Cheryl said. "Ozzy and I can put the sleds away."

Robyn and Darby hustled about the yard as he and Cheryl finished putting away the teams and hung the harnesses in the little barn. Floodlights illuminated the dog yard, and the two young women efficiently distributed dog food, meat, and fresh water to the forty-odd dogs currently in Robyn's care.

Cheryl showed him where to stow his light sled, and they left the barn together. "How about that hot chocolate?" she asked. "I need to check the stew, too, but I'm ready to relax for a few minutes."

"Sounds good." He followed her in through the back door of the house. He'd only been here a couple of times, with Rick. The kitchen smelled great, and it looked more modern and better equipped than the one in his cabin.

Grandpa Steve stood in the dining room doorway. "There you are, Cheryl. Did Robby tell you I'm going over to her place with her?"

"Yes, she did."

"Did she tell you why?"

"No." Cheryl eyed him as she might a toddler who never ceased asking questions. "Why are you going?"

"To get your Christmas present." Grandpa's face beamed. "Robby's been hiding it for me for almost a month over there."

Cheryl laughed. "And here I thought you'd forgotten to get me anything."

"Oh no. Never." Steve turned to Oz, still grinning. "She's a good girl, but it's hard to keep secrets from her. She cleans everything, so I have to find ways to hide stuff I don't want her to see. How you been, Doc?" He held out his hand, and Oz shook it, laughing.

"Great. Sounds like you've found a good solution to hiding presents. How are you doing, Mr. Holland?"

"Steve. Call me Steve. I'm doing good."

Cheryl lifted the lid of a Crock-Pot, which sent a mouth-watering wave of steam billowing. "We're going to have some cocoa, Dad. Do you want to join us?"

"Is there time, before Robyn's ready to go?"

"I think so. I'll make sure it's not too hot, so you can drink it quicker." She bustled about, setting out mugs and powdered hot chocolate mix.

"Can I help with anything?" Oz asked.

"No thanks. I'm all set. Why don't you and Dad go sit in the living room? Oh, if he doesn't have the fire going, you can start that."

Oz followed the old man through the dining room. The table was set with gleaming china. A brass bowl in the middle held huge pine cones and red Christmas tree balls. In the living room, a plump Christmas tree stood sentinel over a mound of wrapped packages near the wall opposite the fireplace.

"Have a seat." Steve centered himself before an armchair and sank slowly into it.

A blaze flickered low on the hearth. "Mind if I add a couple of sticks?" Oz asked.

"Go right ahead, young man."

Oz bent to pick two short logs from the woodbox. "Did you

build this house, sir?"

"What? Oh no. Danny and I bought it when we first came here. A family had it, but they were pulling up stakes. Danny and Cheryl had Aven. That's Robyn's brother. Robby was born here. Well, not here. At the hospital in Anchorage. But we've been here more than twenty-five years."

Oz stirred the half-burned wood and added his logs then took a seat nearby. "That's a long time. Any regrets?"

"Not a one. Well, of course I could wish that my wife had lived to come up here with us, or that Danny had survived the—" Steve broke off and waved one hand. "That's in the past. No, I don't have any regrets. This is a good place to live and raise kids. Dogs, too."

Cheryl came in carrying a tray. She stopped before Steve. "There you go. Take your 'Grandpa' mug."

Steve laughed and reached for it. "Aven gave me this at Christmas about twenty years ago. I'm amazed I haven't broken it yet."

They sat chatting and sipping their chocolate. The firelight glinted off Cheryl's short brown curls. In the soft lighting, she looked younger than her fifty-plus years.

"So far I feel pretty good this year," Steve said. "Now, last year, that was a different story. They thought I'd had it."

"Oh, Dad, that's not true." Cheryl shook her head and turned to Oz. "He did give us a scare last year, but he's been doing very well. I'm proud of the way he's helped Robyn with the dogs this fall." She looked back at her father-in-law. "You've made a lot of progress. Getting out and exercising has a lot to do with that. I'm so glad you're feeling well."

"I wouldn't say I always feel well," Steve cautioned. "I've got some arthritis, for sure. But I can still get around with a bucket of dog chow, and on a good day I can buckle a harness strap. Thank God for modern medicine."

"I don't know how the pioneers did it," Oz said.

"Isn't that the truth." Steve sipped his cocoa.

Robyn entered through the kitchen. "Hey, Grandpa, are you ready to go? The dogs are all settled for the night, and Darby's gone home."

"I'm ready." Steve set his mug aside and reached for her hand. He let out a low groan as Robyn helped pull him up out of his chair.

Oz stood, too.

"We ought to get you one of those chairs that lifts you up," Robyn said to her grandfather.

"No, don't." Cheryl frowned at her over her mug. "The more he does on his own, the better. If you make it too easy for him, he won't be able to do anything."

"Oh, you're cruel," Steve said, leaning on Robyn's arm as he shuffled toward the coat closet. "You'll make me keep working in the kennel till I can't get out of bed."

Having just heard him claim he was still good for a day's work, Oz laughed at the old man's play for sympathy.

"Ha!" Cheryl said. "We couldn't keep you out of the dog yard if we wanted to."

"Mom's right. And I couldn't get along without you." Robyn took his jacket from the closet and held it for him.

"I'll expect you two and Rick back here in an hour or so," Cheryl said.

When Robyn and Steve had left, they sat in silence for a moment.

"I understand your son and his family will arrive tomorrow," Oz said.

"Yes. Aven could only squeeze out two days, but they're coming." Cheryl's smile lit her whole face. "I can't wait to hold my little grandson again."

"Will I see them at church?"

"I doubt they'll arrive until noon or later, but you'll join us for dinner, won't you?"

"Oh, I don't want to intrude. You were gracious to include me in your family time tonight, but—"

"No buts, Oswald. You're far from home, and we want you with us."

He laughed at her unexpected use of his first name.

She leaned forward and scowled at him as she had her father-in-law. "Unless you have plans elsewhere, we'll expect you here."

"All right, I give up. I'm sure there won't be a finer table spread in Wasilla."

She relaxed and sank back in her chair. "It will be informal, but I think I can guarantee good food and fellowship."

"What more could a man ask?" He caught her gaze, and they sat looking at each other for a long moment. The fire snapped.

"What about your family, Oz? I know your parents are gone. Don't you have siblings?"

He shook his head. "I had a brother, but he died when. . ." He cleared his throat, suddenly fighting tears. "He died in a motorcycle wreck when he was twenty-five."

"I'm so sorry."

They slid into silence again, watching the fire. Was this the time to tell her about Jo? Maybe not. Things had already gone mournful, and he wasn't comfortable with that. Besides, Rick had probably clued her in already that he'd lost his wife. She'd never asked, which made him think she knew at least the basics. He didn't want to discuss it now. Time spent with Cheryl should be full of peace and contentment, with a spark of hope.

After a minute, he stirred. "Let's not get all gloomy. This is going to be a wonderful holiday."

She reached for her mug. "Yes. I've been blessed, seeing my children start their families. And Dad—he's really come a great way since last year. I'm so thankful."

"Cheryl. . ."

"Yes?" She looked at him, a tentative smile hovering at her lips.

"I had a lot of fun today."

"So did I."

"I wondered. . ." He paused then shrugged off his own reservations. "I wondered if you would consider going on the trip
with me in March. The one where we'll use ground transportation and tag the bear cubs."

Her jaw dropped. She sat staring at him, holding her mug
in both hands.

"Me? You're asking *me*?"

"Yes."

"But. . .I am *so* not qualified."

"I think you are."

"Didn't you tell me that all the other people on the trip will
be scientists?"

"Yes, but—"

"Are they bringing along secretaries?"

"Uh. . ." He gritted his teeth. "I don't know. Probably not."

She shifted in her chair and set the mug down. "Wouldn't
you rather have another vet along? Someone who knows about
bear biology and habitat and all that?"

"No."

That silenced her. His face suddenly warmed, more so than
he could account for from the heat of the fire or his beard. "I'm
not sure exactly who is going, other than Michael Torrence and
Annette Striker. They're geologists. I met them on my Russian
trip. Their job will be taking core samples from the ice sheet."

"Annette? So, there'll be at least one other woman along."

"Yes. I wouldn't ask you to go if it were all men."

"But why? Why me and not some grad student or another
zoologist?"

"Because I think you'd be an asset to my project. We work
well together, and you've already shown you're willing to save
my bacon if I fall into a snow bank."

She chuckled, and a knot in his chest unraveled.

"I just don't know what to say. I feel so inadequate."

"Think about it." He sat forward and held her gaze. "I need someone else with me—it's a two-person job. It's true I could ask for someone from the university or the big veterinary hospital where Rick used to work in Anchorage. There are probably a dozen qualified people who'd jump at the chance to go. If you decide you really don't want to, I'll start putting out feelers. But I'd rather take someone who understands the way I work and who can read my handwriting."

She laughed again. The battle was nearly won.

He said quickly, "Besides, if you say no, my Christmas gift is wasted."

"What? You're crazy! What Christmas gift are you talking about?"

"It's out in my truck."

"Well." She eyed him pensively. "I guess it's a good thing I got you something."

They both laughed, and it felt good to share the moment with her—a moment that held no sadness, only satisfaction and a bit of speculation. The trip would be business, but it would also be a test of their friendship. Could she see that? He thought she could.

Cheryl's eyes narrowed suddenly and she stood. "Come on into the kitchen. I need to put the biscuits in the oven."

He followed her, carrying their empty mugs, and leaned on the counter, watching her work.

She washed her hands and deftly combined the flour, shortening, milk, and baking powder into a spongy dough. She flopped it out of the bowl and kneaded it rhythmically on a butcher block. "How are you doing with the light deprivation?" she asked.

He looked up from her hands into her eyes. "Good. At least, I think so. Getting out in the sunlight helps. Like today. I didn't feel at all depressed, if you don't count the moment I realized

I'd let my dog team get away."

"There's hope for you then."

How big a role did Cheryl play in his lack of melancholia? Quite a lot, unless he was mistaken. "Of course, the winter is young. What about you? Do you feel blue in the winter?"

"Sometimes." She gave a little laugh and tossed her head. "But then, sometimes I get that way in summer, too, so it's probably not Seasonal Affective Disorder."

"That's understandable. You've been through a lot."

She pressed her lips together and avoided his gaze while she patted the dough into a thick round on her breadboard. She opened a drawer beneath the counter and took out a biscuit cutter. Swiftly she cut a dozen circles from the dough and popped them into a pan. When she lifted the pan and held it out, Oz straightened. "Would you please put this in the oven?" She looked up at him. Her eyes glistened.

And he'd been so determined not to let past griefs color their day. "Cheryl, I'm sorry if I—"

"I'm okay."

He nodded and took the pan of biscuits. The oven was already hot, and he slid it in, onto the rack in the center, and closed the door.

Behind him, she said, "I just. . .you know. Sometimes I think about Dan. Holidays are hard. But I'm thankful for what God has given me. For a while, I wasn't sure Robyn and Dad and I could stay here. Things were tight after the insurance money ran out. But you know, God never forgets His children."

Oz stepped over close to her. "That's true. I'm glad you've felt His care."

She nodded and ducked her head again as she shaped the remaining dough. "I shouldn't have brought it up. No sense going into the sad widow mode and bringing you into the morass."

He sucked in a deep breath. "Look, since we're being frank, there's something you should know. I don't really want to tell you, because I pictured this day as a happy time, without any gloom and doom. But if we're going to. . . Well, I guess I should lay everything on the table."

She raised her eyebrows, her hands still on the dough. "You don't have to tell me anything."

"I. . ." He'd almost said, "I want to," but that wasn't true. If his conscience would let him, he'd never tell her. But the time seemed right, and he knew he'd feel guilty if he didn't. "It's just a matter of record. I wasn't totally honest about why I changed careers. I was married. For two years. Way back, before I knew Rick."

Silence hung between them for about five seconds.

Cheryl picked up her biscuit cutter. "I knew you'd been married, but. . . Okay. Why did you go to vet school?"

"It's true I'd always wanted to be a veterinarian. But Jo—my wife—served on the police force in Buffalo, and she was killed while she was on duty. I. . .decided to get out of the line I was in. I couldn't take it anymore, going into the jail every day and seeing men there who'd committed crimes and felt no remorse whatsoever. Before Jo's death, I was able to keep it in perspective, but when I became a victim. . ." He sighed. "I took some time off, and then I decided to go back to school."

"I'm so sorry."

He nodded, not looking at her.

She wiped her floury hands on a dish towel and touched his arm. "Ozzy. . ."

He swallowed hard and turned his gaze on her troubled face.

"Are you sure you're ready. . . ? I mean, it's not like we've been dating or anything, but—"

"Today was a date. Wasn't it? It was for me."

She nodded slowly. "Yes, it was for me, too. My first date in thirty years. But if you'd prefer not to think of it that way. . ."

His throat ached, and he moved turtle-like to cover her hand with his. "I do want to think of it that way. It's been more than ten years since she died. It's been tough, but yes, I'm ready to move on. What about you? It wasn't so long ago that Dan died."

"No. Four years is all. It seems like yesterday. And a hundred years ago."

He wanted to pull her into his arms, but he held back. Better to go slowly and prayerfully. Instead of rushing into something they'd both regret later, maybe they could ease their friendship into something stronger. He squeezed her hand and released it. "I know exactly what you mean. Thank you."

She sniffed. "I actually feel better, now that we've talked about it."

Oz was able to smile then. "I do, too."

While she cleaned up the counter, he slipped out to his truck and retrieved the packages he'd prepared for the family and slid them under the Christmas tree. He'd either settled on the perfect thing for Cheryl or a hopelessly wrong thing.

A few minutes later, Rick, Robyn, and Steve breezed in, and they sat down to supper. During the blessing, Oz once again felt a part of the family circle as Steve and Cheryl gripped his hands. They all included him in the conversation and told him some of their holiday traditions. But when they gathered about the tree, Oz began to feel out of place. He should have begged off.

The gifts that the Bakers and Hollands presented to each other were not extravagant, other than the new dog Rick had purchased for Robyn. He brought it in from the kennel with a huge red bow about its neck.

After they'd all exclaimed over its fine points, however, Cheryl banished it to the dog yard. "Huskies are not house dogs."

"Okay, Mom." Robyn took it out with good grace and returned to distribute more gifts.

Grandpa seemed pleased with the box of dried fruit Oz had

ordered for him, and Cheryl obviously loved the new food processor she found in Steve's package for her.

Oz opened a small gift box from Cheryl and discovered a high-quality compass inside. He assured her it would come in handy on his dog sled runs and snowmobile trips. He tucked it into his pocket, knowing it would travel with him to the North Slope, even if she didn't. Rick and Robyn gave him a wool sweater with Native Alaskan designs knit in. From Steve he received a book on Alaskan history.

Rick handed Oz's package to Cheryl. He found himself holding his breath.

She carefully removed the paper and smiled. "Thank you. This seems significant." She held up the two books on polar bear habitat and anatomy so the others could see them.

He longed to explain his reasoning to her and tell her that they were readable yet scholarly treatments and that he didn't want to pressure her, but he thought she'd love the experience if she went.

Instead he just sat there, watching her face. The smile never quite left her mouth as she showed the books around. When she handed them to Rick for a moment, she looked over at Oz. She nodded slowly, thoughtfully, gazing into his eyes.

"Thanks." She only mouthed it, but he gathered in the single word and hoarded it. She liked his choice. And she was thinking about going with him.

He exhaled and winked at her. Cheryl laughed like a giddy bobbysoxer, and Oz knew irrevocably—he would never again leave Alaska for long. He was staying. Oh yes, this was home.

eight

"There's a wolf down there on top of the mountain." The flight instructor, Clyde Hart, pointed out the side window of the plane. "Bank around so you can see him."

"Uh. . .okay." Oz thought about what the simple maneuver entailed. It was only his third lesson in the dual-control Cessna, but he loved the freedom he felt soaring above the frozen landscape. They'd flown up the Knik Glacier and were heading back to the Palmer airport now, where Clyde kept his plane.

Half a minute later, Oz had turned and headed back over the rocky mountaintop. The barren summit was covered with snow, except where outcroppings of rock thrust upward. The dark animal stood out in stark relief, trotting across the white expanse.

Oz had seen wolves before, on his Siberian and Canadian research trips, but usually in clusters around a kill. He'd never seen one traveling alone in the wild before. "Cool. So, what now?"

"We'd better get home before it gets dark," Clyde said. "Unfortunately, this time of year flying hours are limited."

"When can we go up again?" Oz asked. He banked again and spotted Pioneer Peak off to his left. Palmer straight ahead. Now that the Hollands' mid-January sled dog race was over, he had his Saturdays free.

"How about next week, same time, if the weather's okay? We'll be able to stay up a little longer."

Oz nodded. "Good. I'll call you the day before to confirm."

He radioed in to the small airport. Another plane had just landed, but there was no other incoming traffic at the moment. His heart thudded as he squared up for the runway. This was always the scariest part. The adrenaline spurted every time he got ready to land.

"Relax," Clyde said. "You're doing great. Check your rpm's."

Oz eased the throttle back and moved the yoke forward a little to keep the air speed above a stall. His gaze darted over the controls. Everything right? He could still power up and go around. No, it looked good. He nosed up just a hair to drop the speed and held the plane straight, holding his breath. The wheels hit the runway all at once and he exhaled.

"Perfect." Clyde slapped his shoulder. "Just like a surgeon. I find you medical guys are all precise. Everything's just so on the landing or you abort and try again."

Oz applied the brakes as the Cessna rolled down the runway.

"Next time we'll do some touch-and-go landings," Clyde said. "After you've done a bunch of those, you won't be so nervous coming in."

"If you say so. I love flying. I just hate landing."

"That's going to keep you super careful. When you've got twenty hours or so under your belt, you'll stop dreading the landing and be able to enjoy the ride more."

On the drive from Palmer back to Wasilla, Oz turned his truck's headlights on. A rim of pink still iced the mountains in the west. He put on his headset and called Cheryl. "Hey, it's Oz. Any messages for me today?"

"No emergencies. Cathy Sennett would like you to call her about her quarter horse's leg."

"Something wrong? I thought he was getting better."

"I don't think so, but she needs reassurance."

Oz glanced at his watch. "Maybe I can run out there now and take a quick look. I told her he'll need a couple of weeks of rest though. I hope she hasn't ridden him yet."

"Okay. And I scheduled two barn calls for you on Monday morning. I put them into the computer."

"Great. You should be relaxing on Saturday. Sounds like

you're working as hard at home as you would in the office."

"It's okay." Cheryl hesitated. "How did your lesson go?"

"Terrific. We flew up the glacier, and we saw a wolf. We're going to practice more landings next week. Not my favorite part, but arguably the most important."

"Right. Well, I'll see you in church tomorrow."

Oz signed off, thinking that her voice sounded small and compressed. Maybe she was tired. He'd have to talk to Rick about Cheryl's extra work. Clients shouldn't be calling her at home. Maybe they could route the veterinary office's phone line to his or Rick's cell phone on weekends. That would keep Cheryl from feeling she had to keep working 24/7.

࣌

Cheryl sat for a long time at her desk on the evening of Friday, February 24, reconciling her bank statement and going over the financial records for Robyn's kennel business. The hoopla of the Fire & Ice race, sponsored by Holland Kennel each year, was a month behind them, and Robyn had paid off the last of the bills related to the event. Cheryl had kept the books for the business since the family started it. Maybe it was time Robyn took over or hired the accountant Rick used for the veterinary practice.

The back door opened. She felt the cold draft as Robyn and her grandfather came in from the dog yard.

"Do you want some coffee?" she called.

"Not me." Steve hobbled into the living room. "I'm beat. Think I'll lie down and watch a little TV."

"Are you all right?"

"Did I say I wasn't?" He kept going down the hall.

Cheryl watched his gait critically then swiveled to look at Robyn. "Is he really okay?"

"I think so. Just tired. He helped me clean out the dog pens. I mean, he really helped, not just supervised."

"Aha. Then it's probably just as well if he goes to bed early." Cheryl stood and stretched. "I finished going over your accounts.

You did well on the race this year." She handed Robyn her open ledger. "Here's your bottom line. Not bad."

"Super. We had the biggest field ever for the Fire & Ice, and a lot of people entered the short races, too. More sponsors and vendors than ever before." Robyn sat down on the arm of the sofa. "Thanks for doing that, Mom. It's a big help."

"I was thinking maybe you should ask David Hill to do your books. You've got him preparing your tax returns anyway. Your business is solidly in the black. I think you can afford it."

Robyn cocked her head to one side. "I suppose you're right. Like Grandpa, I'm slow to make changes."

"Only in some things. The changes you've made in the breeding end of the business are good ones. And I just thought that, since I'm working full time now, it might be a good time to make the transition."

"I'll talk to Rick about it. And, Mom, I appreciate all the work you've put in over the years."

"I know you do, honey." Cheryl slipped into the recliner opposite her.

"So. . .Ozzy's leaving Monday for his research trip."

"Yes. He's looking forward to it." Cheryl tried not to let her dismay show on her face.

"Are you upset that he's leaving? He'll only be gone two weeks."

"No. This is part of why he came here. They hope to catch and tag a lot of polar bears. It's just. . ."

"What, Mom?" Robyn leaned toward her, frowning. "I know you and Oz have gotten close."

"We're good friends," Cheryl said quickly.

"Sure. We'll all miss him." Robyn eyed her speculatively. "Mom, you care about him a lot, don't you?"

Cheryl licked her dry lips. It seemed a bit strange to have her daughter questioning her as to where her affections lay. But she'd always been open with Robyn, and being coy wouldn't help.

Her potential romance with Oz had seemed to stall for a few weeks after Christmas, in the whirl of preparations for the Fire & Ice. Oz had pitched in to help like a member of the family, but they hadn't had much quiet time together. He'd taken her out to dinner once since, but when all was said and done, their relationship hadn't progressed much. Now he was working toward his pilot's license. As the daylight hours increased, it seemed he spent every spare hour with his flight instructor.

"Yes, I do. I guess that's why I'm a little on edge."

Robyn's dark eyes focused on her sharply. "It's because he's flying to Barrow, isn't it? Not that he's going away, but that he's *flying* away. Like Dad did."

Cheryl's stomach twisted. "Honey, you mustn't say a word." Tears sprang to her eyes and colored her voice.

Robyn rose and stepped over to her chair. She stooped and slid her arm around her mother's shoulders. "It's going to be okay, Mom," she whispered.

Cheryl nodded and waved her hand helplessly. "I know. I feel so silly. Because I *do* trust God."

"He'll protect Ozzy."

"Yes."

Robyn hesitated then went to her knees on the braided rug beside the chair. "Mom, I know it's hard, but we need to remember, even if something happens, God is still in control."

Cheryl nodded and squeezed her hand. "I know. It's just remembering that night. Waiting and not knowing. And getting the call." Her tears splashed down her cheeks. "I try not to worry when he's having a flight lesson. In fact, I've purposely avoided knowing exactly when he's having them."

"But having his license will be a big help to him. He likes flying, and he'll be able to get around so much easier. Of course, he won't be the one flying the plane on his research trip."

"No, but then your father wasn't the pilot when his plane went down either." Cheryl clenched her hands. "I'm not sure

I could take it if Oz's plane went down. And once they get to Barrow, they're going to take a helicopter out every day, if the weather allows it. Every single day."

Robyn's wan smile didn't reassure her. "I know. I guess it's a good thing Oz asked you to go on the later trip, not this one. You'll have to fly up there with him, but you'll be using snow machines once you get there, not a helicopter."

Cheryl shook her head. "I don't think it would worry me as much if I were with him. If he went down, so would I. And I wouldn't be back here wondering."

Robyn drew back and raised her eyebrows. "What? You're not afraid to fly, but you're afraid to let someone you love get in an aircraft? That doesn't make sense."

"When have I ever made sense?"

"Aw, come on. You're very efficient and practical. Rick says you're the best office manager he's ever known."

Cheryl managed a shaky smile. "It was wonderful of him and Oz to raise my wages at the first of the year. But I'll still worry about Oz doing all that flying, I'm afraid. And it'll be worse when he gets his pilot's license."

Robyn chuckled. "Mom, think about it. This isn't going away. What are you going to do if he buys his own airplane?"

"Do you think he will? He and Rick aren't clearing that much in the practice yet, are they?"

"I know they turned a solid profit for the year. Business is good."

"I'm glad for them. But. . .how would you feel if Rick bought a plane and started flying all the time?"

Robyn sobered. "I'm not sure. But the first thing I'd do would be to tell him if it bothered me. I'd talk out with him what happened to Dad and how it scares me a little to think. . .to think I could lose him that way, too."

"You're reading my mind, aren't you?" Cheryl studied her and reached to brush back a strand of her daughter's dark hair. "You look like your father, but you're so like me inside. I'm sorry about that."

"Don't be. I admire you. You've got spunk."

"Thanks. I think. But you're stronger than I am. Tougher."

Robyn inhaled deeply. "You really ought to tell Ozzy how you feel about him flying."

"No." She said it so quickly, Robyn's eyebrows shot up. "I can't do that to him—send him away knowing I'll fret about it."

"Okay, I'll tell you what. How about if you decide not to fret about it?"

Cheryl looked away. "Yeah. That's my goal. Psalm 37. I read it this morning, and I intend to read it every day while he's gone, to remind me not to worry. Because I know God doesn't want me to do that."

"Right. Maybe I'll come over to the practice every day at lunchtime. You and Rick and I can pray and eat lunch together. Angela, too, if she wants."

"That sounds good."

"But you won't tell Oz?"

Cheryl clamped her lips together and shook her head.

"You'd feel better if you did."

"No, I wouldn't. And he'd feel worse. He'd worry about me worrying." She stood and embraced her daughter. "Thanks, honey. I'm going to trust God in this—not just to keep Oz safe, but to keep me grounded, no matter what happens."

"All right. And I'll do everything I can to distract you. If I catch you biting your nails even once, I'll slap you silly."

❧

"Guess I'd better get going." Oz grinned at Cheryl and Rick, unable to contain his anticipation.

Rick stuck out his hand. "We'll miss you."

"Thanks." Oz shook it and turned to face Cheryl.

"You won't decide you love it so much above the Arctic Circle that you won't come back, will you?" Her long lashes hid her eyes, but her lips twitched, holding back a smile.

"I hardly think so. We've gained a lot of daylight hours here, but I've got to regress to darkness at noon."

"You'll have some daylight up there, won't you?" she asked.

"Oh yeah, I was exaggerating. That's why they scheduled the trip now, not in January—not enough light then to make it worthwhile."

Rick smiled. "I guess it would be pretty hard to track the bears in the dark."

"Yeah, we're planning on six hours or more a day."

"We'll be thinking of you. Good luck spotting the bears," Rick said.

"We'll be praying for you, too." Cheryl's quiet tone made him focus on her. She'd set her jaw as though determined not to say anything out of line.

"Walk to my truck with me?" he asked softly.

"Sure. Let me grab my jacket."

She left the room and Oz put on his coat.

"We'll see you soon, buddy." He gave Rick a nod and walked down the hallway, pulling on his gray gloves. Angela was settling in at the front desk. She would free Cheryl up to assist Rick more during Oz's absence.

"Good-bye, Dr. Thormond," she called.

"See you, Angela." He nodded to the two pet owners sitting in the waiting area. One held a small plastic cage on her lap, and the other sat with a magazine on his lap and a malamute sprawled at his feet.

Cheryl met Oz at the door, and they walked across the parking lot together. At his truck, they stopped, and he faced her.

"I'm going to miss you."

She smiled. "Thanks. I know I'll be thinking of you a lot and praying for you."

"That's nice. Thank you." A sharp wind cut down through the valley. She hadn't put her hat on, and it lifted her curls and ruffled his beard. No sense prolonging the parting in the icy cold, but still. . . "It's been kind of crazy the last few weeks, getting ready for my trip and all."

"That's understandable."

"I hope we can find some time together after I get back. I'd like to spend time with you and. . .maybe just talk." The flying lessons had eaten up a lot of his time. It had seemed logical to take advantage of good weather, but it meant he hadn't spent the time with Cheryl that he wanted to. There was so much he didn't know about her.

She nodded, her brown eyes huge in her face. "I'd like that."

"Good." He almost wished he'd asked her to take him to the airport. Then she could meet him there when he returned, the way she had the first time he met her. But he'd already told them he'd drive his truck and leave it in long-term parking. She'd be waiting here when he got back to Wasilla. He smiled down at her. "I'll send you a postcard."

That brought a chuckle. "I'd hold you to it, but I doubt they have postcards there. You'll be lucky if mail goes out at all during your stay."

"Ooo, I hope the weather's not that bad."

"Me, too." She went all sober again.

"Hey, you're not going to worry about me, are you?"

"No. I'm definitely not doing that. You've got the best security net in the universe."

"You've got that right."

"And besides, I have a lot more reading to do. I'm really getting into this polar bear thing."

"That's terrific. I'm glad you decided to go next month."

She shivered.

He'd better leave so she could go in out of the cold. He wanted to kiss her, but that seemed a bit premature. He reached out a gloved hand.

She'd shoved her bare hands into her coat pockets, but she

pulled one out and squeezed his fingers.

Oz looked down at the black *H* she'd inked on the back of his left glove. They had so many memories to finish. "*H* for hug." He pulled her into a quick embrace. When he released her, she was smiling. Not the shy, secret smile. The big, joyful one. "Bye." He climbed into the truck.

She stood back and waved as he drove away toward the George Parks Highway.

᷾

On Friday morning the mailman brought a bundle of letters and a package to the door of the clinic and handed them to Cheryl. Snow fell outside, and she wondered how the weather was behaving seven hundred miles to the north.

She put the mail down on the desk where Angela sat and then turned to the waiting clients. "Dr. Baker is ready to see Cinnamon."

A middle-aged man lifted a cat carrier and followed her down the hall to Rick's treatment room. Rick greeted them and asked the man to set the carrier on the exam table. Cheryl closed the door so that the cat couldn't get away if it leaped off the table.

Ten minutes later, after Rick had vaccinated the cat and pre-scribed an ointment for a patch of eczema on its face, Cheryl walked with the owner to the front desk. "Good-bye, Mr. Allen. I'm sure Cinnamon will feel better soon, but be sure to call us if she doesn't."

"Thanks." He pulled out his checkbook.

She was about to turn away when Angela said, "Oh, Cheryl, there's some personal mail for you here."

Curious, Cheryl took the item Angela held out—a color postcard. "Thank you." Her heart fluttered as she walked quickly to the restroom and closed the door. The photo depicted bril-liant green Northern Lights in full display over a rustic village. She turned it over and glanced first at the signature. Ozzy. She laughed aloud and read the message. He'd compressed his usually flowing script to fit the meager space allowed.

> *Hey, Cheryl!*
> *You were wrong—they do have postcards here. This is Nuwuk, an Inupiat fishing village out on Point Barrow. We're socked in today with snow but yesterday collared five bears & tagged three yearlings. 17 below zero. See ya.*
> *Ozzy*

She read it over again and held it to her chest as tears filled her eyes. Not very romantic, but she didn't care. The fact that he'd bothered to find a postcard and managed to get it to her, probably by way of the first outgoing plane, meant more than a bouquet of hothouse roses would have.

"Thank You, Lord." She wiped away her tears and hurried to Rick's office to show it to him before taking the next patient in.

nine

Ten days later, Oz collected his luggage off the carousel in the Anchorage airport. Too bad home was still an hour away. Again he wished Cheryl was there, eyeing him cautiously and mumbling to herself.

He smiled at the memory. She'd worked her way to the top of his "Ten Reasons to Stay in Alaska" list, with polar bears and working with Rick vying for a close second.

Heading out of the airport, he passed displays of mounted Alaskan wildlife and native artwork. He paused before a case of jade and ivory jewelry. Wouldn't that beaded necklace look great on Cheryl? He'd have to give her a place to wear it, other than church. She didn't wear a lot of jewelry to the office. He squinted at the price tag. On the other hand, he could take her out to dinner about ten times for that amount. He tugged his roller suitcase over toward the wall and found a niche out of the foot traffic.

Taking out his cell phone, he punched in the number for the clinic. Probably Angela would answer.

"Baker Animal Hospital."

He grinned so hard his face hurt.

A passing woman glanced at him and raised her eyebrows as she walked on.

"Cheryl. It's Oz. I'm in Anchorage."

"Thank God!"

"How are you?"

"I'm great. We've all been praying for you. And we have a long list of non-urgent patients for you to see tomorrow if you can."

"I'll be ready." He glanced at his watch. "Can I see you

tonight? By the time I drive to Wasilla, it'll be too late to come to the office."

"I'd love to see you. How about supper with me and Steve? Around six-thirty?"

"Sounds good."

ză

Cheryl set the dining table for two. She did it every night, but this time she used her best china and set new candles in her brass holders. Should she light them before dinner, or would that be a bit much?

Robyn came in through the kitchen. "Wow, pretty snazzy. Where's Grandpa?"

"In his recliner. Thanks for having him over tonight."

Robyn laughed. "He wanted to stay and yak with Ozzy, but I think I finally got the message across that he can do that another time. You and Oz need some time alone."

Cheryl's cheeks warmed. "Oh, I don't know. . ."

"Stow it, Mom. I'm not buying it."

"But I told Oz on the phone that Grandpa Steve would be with us."

"Oh, and you think Ozzy will be horrified when he discovers that plan went awry and it's just the two of you?" Robyn laughed and walked through to the living room.

Cheryl surveyed the table in dismay. Was she making too much of this? Should she insist that Steve stay here and eat with her and Oz? Their friendship was solid, and she wanted it to remain that way. Would this look like a setup?

She snatched the tapers off the table and placed them on the windowsill. No candlelight. Maybe she should use her old ironstone dishes instead of the china.

Robyn and Steve came in. Steve had his jacket, hat, and mittens on.

"What are you doing?" Robyn asked, eyeing the plates Cheryl held in her hands. "Unsetting the table?"

"I decided it was too much. I'm going with the everyday dishes."

"You are not." Robyn wrested the plates from her and set them gently back on the table. "Hey! Where have those romantic candles run off to?"

"Oh, honey, I'm so nervous. Oz expects a nice, homey supper with me and your grandpa, and it will look like I've prettied up my spider lair for him and gotten rid of the chaperone. I don't want him to think I'm chasing him."

"Mom! You've got to stop this." Robyn stared at her. "You honestly believe he'll think you're vamping him?"

Cheryl grabbed the back of the nearest chair. Her cheeks felt as if they'd caught fire. "Well, I. . ." She clapped her hands to her face.

"Now, Cheryl, Oz Thormond is a sensible man. He's not going to get the wrong idea." Steve laid his hand on her shoulder. "You just relax and have a nice evening."

While he spoke, Robyn spotted the candles and swooped on them. She situated them precisely on the table. "There. Don't you dare take those off again."

Cheryl exhaled. "All right."

"And, Mom? Go put a dress on."

"What? No. That's silly. He won't—"

"A dress," Robyn repeated. "Come on, Grandpa. Let's vamoose."

Cheryl watched them out the door and looked down at her black slacks and powder blue sweater. Should she change? That smacked of overkill.

The front door opened, and Robyn stuck her head back inside. "What are you waiting for? Go get dressed. The green jacket dress. Now."

❧

Oz checked his appearance in the mirror and ran a comb through his hair. When did he get so gray? Maybe spending the last two weeks in sub-zero temperatures had done something to his hair. At least he didn't have to shave. His beard had come in full, almost lush. He rather liked it.

He looked down at his plain blue shirt. Maybe he ought to wear woodsman flannel. He didn't want Cheryl to feel uncomfortable if he came to supper overdressed.

His phone rang, and he snatched it off his dresser.

"Oz?"

"Yes?"

"This is Robyn. Welcome back."

"Thanks. How's everything?"

"Terrific. Are you headed to Mom's for supper?"

"Yes, I was just about to leave."

"Wear a tie."

He hesitated. "I beg your pardon."

"A tie. You know, those things men wear around their necks when they want to convince you they're civilized."

"That's what I thought you said. Are you sure?"

"Trust me on this one. Wear a tie."

"O. . .kay." He signed off and dashed to the closet. What was going on? Would Steve wear a tie to supper? Or did Robyn have something up her sleeve? Maybe the reporter from the weekly paper was coming to interview him about his research and she wanted him to look presentable for photos.

He picked the tie he'd worn with this shirt for the *Scientific American* interview. Should he wear a jacket, too? Robyn had been rather vague. He considered calling her back and demanding to know what was up. Was a tie enough for Alaska formal? Just in case, he snatched his corduroy sports jacket. Okay. Not bad at all.

He grabbed his parka, phone, and keys, along with a small bag from the airport shop where he'd finally decided on a gift for Cheryl.

At the Hollands' house, he parked his truck and picked up

the small bag off the passenger seat. He took out the box and tucked it into his pocket. The big log house beckoned him with warm light spilling from the living room's front windows. Cheryl's car was the only vehicle in the yard, so this wasn't a press party. Good.

As he knocked on the front door, doubts again swept over him. What if Cheryl and Steve were kicking back in jeans? They'd think he was citified for sure. And they had to know he didn't come in from Barrow dressed like a college professor. Could he peel off the sports jacket and toss it in the truck before he went in?

Too late. The door swung open. Cheryl stood in the opening with soft light glowing behind her and her smile radiating welcome. "Oz. I'm so glad you're back. Come in."

She stepped aside and he entered, unable to take his eyes off her. The muted green dress she wore had simple lines but suited her perfectly. Around her neck hung a thin gold chain holding an oval locket. Her curls pouffed gently about her face, but it was those brown eyes that captivated him.

He reached for her hand. "You look terrific."

"Thanks. I hope you're hungry."

"Starved."

"Good. I made chicken pie." She took his parka and hung it in the closet near the door. Her glance swept over him, and she didn't say anything, but he was pretty sure he saw approval in her eyes and maybe just a tinge of anxiety.

She led him toward the dining room. The savory cooking smells made his mouth water.

"Oh, I should tell you, Robyn hauled her grandfather off for the evening. Sort of last-minute. I didn't know he was going when you called." She glanced over her shoulder at him, her brow slightly wrinkled.

"I'll have to catch up with him soon. He'll want to see some pictures from the trip."

"Yes. He's very interested in the polar bear project." She turned with a smile and a little heave of her breath and touched the back of one chair. "Why don't you sit here, and I'll bring in the food."

"Can I help?"

"Uh. . .well, sure."

He followed her into the kitchen. The tempting chicken pie sat on top of the range, brown and steaming.

She opened the oven and removed a pan of golden biscuits. From the refrigerator, she took a glass bowl of green salad and placed it in his hands. "Can you handle that and a basket of biscuits? I'll bring the pie, and I think that's it."

When they were seated at the table, she gazed at him with the shy, beneath-the-lashes look. "Would you ask the blessing, Oz?"

"Sure." Instinctively, he reached for her hand. She blushed a little and closed her eyes.

"Lord, we thank You for safety and for this food and for the company, major blessings all."

She smiled as she cut into the chicken pie and put a generous slice on his plate. "I'm getting very excited about our trip. Tell me how things went and what we'll focus on next month."

"To be honest, I can't wait to go back. We lost two days, due to weather, but I expected that. In fact, that's a pretty good record. And our tally of bears caught impressed the folks footing the bill with the grant."

"How many did you catch?"

"Nearly a hundred." He took a biscuit and broke it open. The flaky layers looked so tempting that he took a bite without even waiting to butter it. "Mmm, that's good."

"Thanks." Cheryl took some salad and passed him the bowl.

"Of course, a lot of the bears we got hold of were repeats from previous studies, but that's good in some ways. It lets us follow them and add to the data others have already collected on them. We put new collars on twenty-nine adults and tagged twenty of this year's cubs and seven older juveniles no one had caught before."

"Wow. That's a lot, isn't it?"

"It's a good number. With the repeats, we took tissue samples and measurements and recorded where we caught them so the data can be compared with past records. Three of the adults we collared had ear tags."

She nodded. "So, they'd been tagged as cubs, and now they're mature enough to be collared."

"Right." Oz took a bite of the chicken pie. The flavor made him think of childhood and Grandma's and good times. "You are such a good cook, Cheryl."

"Thank you." She blotted her lips with her napkin. "Do the hunters up there take a lot of tagged or collared bears?"

"Yes, quite a few. And they usually turn the equipment in. They know what we're doing can help them in the long run. Learning more about the bears' habits and distribution will help with managing the population. Most of the people are happy to help us."

"And do you think the bear population is shrinking?"

"Not enough evidence so far to be sure. There seem to be a lot in the area we covered. And Alaska has far fewer bears than Canada or Russia."

They ate for a few minutes in silence. Oz began to feel very comfortable as his hunger eased. Cheryl rose and retrieved a pot of coffee from the kitchen. He held out his cup, and she filled it.

"So when you and I go, we'll be going mostly after sows with cubs," she said.

"That's right."

"And we're the only bear people on this trip."

"Yes, the others are doing geological tests. We won't have anyone spotting bears from the air, which could make it a lot harder for us. We'll see. What we want to do is locate some of the females that were collared over the past few years and have given birth this year. We'll get some stats on them and the new cubs."

"Won't they be leaving land for the ice sheet about now?" she asked.

"They're starting now, but the ones with small cubs won't have left when we get there. We can't follow them out onto the ice. For this project, which is totally separate from the one I just came back from, we'll concentrate on maternity dens and new mothers, because we want specific information about the sows and cubs. Enough breeding sows in the area are wearing collars that I think we'll get a good sample. Other organizations who've worked within this bear subpopulation are cooperating. They give us their blessing as far as taking data from animals they tagged. It will help everyone to gather as much information as possible and share it."

"So, we'll send them our findings, and they can incorporate them into their studies, too?"

"Right. It's so hard and so expensive to do research in the Arctic that we have to cooperate whenever we can. The more we all share in the scientific community, the better."

She poured her own cup full of coffee and sat down again. "I'm still amazed that I get to be part of this. I don't feel at all qualified."

"You'll be terrific. And I can't think of anyone else I'd rather have along."

"It's the wildest thing I've ever done, but. . .I can't wait."

He grinned. "I know how you feel. It's going to be great. Just take the best cold-weather gear you can get."

When they'd finished the main course, she pushed her chair back. "I made some rather decadent brownies."

Oz patted his stomach. "Oh, please, no. Maybe later. I'm stuffed."

"Okay. If you're sure."

"This was fantastic."

"Would you like to sit in the living room then? We could take our coffee."

He rose and took his cup with him. She seemed to hesitate in the doorway then sat down on the sofa, hugging one arm tight. That must mean it was up to him—take the recliner opposite or the seat next to her. He compromised and sat down at the other end of the couch and turned to face her.

"You said you have pictures?" she asked.

"Tons. I brought the memory card from my camera, if you want to put it in your computer."

"Oh, let's." She sprang up off the sofa, seeming almost relieved at the prospect of doing something.

They spent the next half hour sitting shoulder-to-shoulder at her desk, with Oz narrating the slide show of his photos. Her questions probed deeply into the techniques they would use on their venture.

"Say, do you know how to shoot?" he asked.

"You mean, shoot a gun? Yes. Dan taught me when we first came here. Do you think I should brush up on that skill?"

"Wouldn't hurt. I mean, just in case. I've never had to shoot a bear with anything but a dart gun, but I did have to do in a wolf once."

She blinked twice and nodded slowly. "Okay."

"Is there a place we could practice safely? I could take you out on Saturday if you'd like."

"Sure. I gave Dan's pistol to my son, but—"

"I'll bring a gun."

"Great." She caught her breath suddenly and turned back toward the monitor.

Oz snaked his arm across the back of her chair. "Maybe right after my flying lesson?"

Her shoulders stiffened and her jaw clenched.

He watched her, confused, waiting for her to relax. Cheryl was so amiable. Surely she wouldn't be offended if he had his pre-scheduled lesson before their shooting date. "I. . .uh. . .set it up with Clyde so that we'll go up as soon as the sun's high enough. Is something wrong?"

"No. No, that's fine."

They sat in silence for a moment. Okay, the schedule wasn't the issue. Was it the mention of her husband that had put a damper on their conversation? Hard to believe that was it, but he couldn't think of any other explanation.

She pulled in a deep breath. "So. There are a few more pictures, right?"

"Yes. Cheryl, are you thinking about Dan?"

She whipped around and stared at him. "How did you know?"

Oz drew back a little, lowering his arm. "It just seemed like after you mentioned him teaching you to shoot that you shut down on me. I'm sorry if I brought up bad memories. You don't have to go shooting with me."

"Oh no, shooting doesn't bother me. I'm fine with that."

"Is it my timing then?"

She shook her head, setting her soft curls dancing, and laid her hand lightly on his sleeve. "No, that's fine. Everything's fine."

He eyed her cautiously. "You sure?"

"Very. And I'd love to do some target practice with you. Just call me Saturday, after you're done. . .done flying."

"Okay." She'd accepted another date with him. He ought to feel happier about it. He could see that she'd loved Dan profoundly. Everything he'd heard from Robyn and Rick bore that out. Could another man live up to those memories?

ten

The Holland family gathered around Cheryl and Oz at the Anchorage airport as they waited to board their plane to Barrow. Several hardy tourists and a few natives of the town would also be on their flight, along with the other scientists.

Cheryl entrusted her boarding pass to Oz and took advantage of the chance to hold her grandson, Axel, before they went through the security line. Her son, Aven, and his wife, Caddie, sat on either side of her, trying to catch up during the hour they had together. The young couple had arranged to make a quick trip up from Kodiak to see her and Oz off, and then would go home with Rick and Robyn to spend a couple of days in Wasilla.

"He's grown so much since Christmas." Cheryl grinned down at the seven-month-old baby.

"He sure has," Aven agreed. "Before you know it, we'll have him out mushing."

Caddie laughed. "Aven wants to get him a puppy already. I said let's wait a year or two."

"Say, Mom, did Dr. Thormond have to get permits to carry all the weapons he's taking?" Aven asked.

"Actually, he's only taking a dart rifle and one pistol, and they're in his checked luggage. The airline personnel are keeping an eye on them. Oz says they're used to people carrying guns for hunting trips and things like that, so he's not worried about it. He plans to buy ammunition for the pistol in Barrow."

Aven nodded. "Sounds good. Sometimes we get to take our personal firearms on deployment, if we're going someplace where we think we might get a chance to do a little hunting."

"Oz took me out a couple of times to practice, so I could use it if need be." Cheryl smiled at the memory of their target shooting. "Oz is an excellent marksman. He surprised me a little bit there." She looked up and saw that he was following their conversation.

"Have to be," Oz said with a grin. "Those tranquilizer darts aren't cheap, and if you miss, it can mean trouble."

"Oh yeah, I wouldn't want to duke it out with a polar bear." Aven eyed his mother with raised eyebrows. "You're the one who surprised me, Mom. When I heard you were going on this expedition, I couldn't believe it. You never liked to go camping in the winter."

Cheryl smiled and bounced Axel gently up and down. "Don't worry about me. We'll have enough gear to keep us comfortable. And I'll put up with a lot to have this experience."

"Yeah," Robyn said, winking conspicuously at her brother. "After all, it's for science."

Oz laughed louder than Cheryl thought was warranted at that, and she felt her face redden.

A bearded man approached them and looked around at Aven, Rick, Oz, and Steve. "Is any of you Dr. Thormond?"

"That would be me." Oz extended his hand.

"Grant Aron. I'm with the geological team on this project."

"Pleased to meet you. Call me Oz. And that lovely lady holding the baby is my assistant, Cheryl Holland. The rest are just riffraff who came to see us off."

They all laughed, and Oz stepped aside with Dr. Aron to discuss details of the trip. A few minutes later he returned to the family group. "Guess we'd better get through security. I know it's hard to leave the rug rat behind."

Cheryl reluctantly handed Axel over to Caddie.

"Have a wonderful time," Caddie said, kissing her cheek.

"Bye, Mom." Aven stooped to kiss her. "We'll be praying for you."

Robyn moved in for a big hug. "You have fun, Mom. I'm so proud of you."

Cheryl squeezed her tight. "Thanks, honey. And you take good care of Grandpa."

"We will."

Neither mentioned the fact that this would be Cheryl's first flight since Dan's crash.

Oz had made the round of handshakes. Cheryl quickly kissed Rick and Steve.

"Now, don't you tangle with those mama bears until they're good and sleepy," Steve said.

She laughed. "Don't worry. We'll be extra careful." She stole an extra second to hug the baby again and snatched up her carry-on.

Oz arched his eyebrows. "All set?"

She gulped, ignoring the forward rolls her stomach was taking. "Yes, sir. Let's do this."

They joined those waiting at the back of the line. Cheryl spotted Grant Aron a short distance ahead of them. As she neared the conveyor belt, she turned for one last wave. Robyn, Rick, and Steve waved. Aven and Caddie were busy gathering the baby's things. Cheryl gulped and stepped forward.

28

Oz looked out the window in his hotel room, but nothing had changed. The snow had begun a half hour before they landed in Barrow. They'd had no trouble landing, though Cheryl had seemed a bit nervous until the plane had come to a stop at the gate. But the storm had escalated into a blizzard that evening, and they'd been stuck in the hotel for two solid days. At least they'd had plenty of time to meet the rest of the scientists and check with the charter helicopter business that would take them to their base camp site. Now they just needed a clear day to get out there and set up the camp.

He paced the limited space in his room and glanced at the clock. Too early for lunch. Back to the window. Theoretically, the sun had risen a couple of hours ago, but the blinding snowfall made it impossible to tell.

His cell phone rang, and he grabbed it from his breast pocket. "Oz."

"Hi. It's Cheryl. Are you as bored as I am?"

"Possibly worse."

She chuckled. "I know this isn't very intellectual, but there's a checkers set down here in the lobby. What do you say?"

"I'll be down in two minutes flat."

"Great. I'll get us some coffee."

When he arrived in the lobby, she was seated in a niche that held two stuffed chairs and a small, square table near a window. She had the promised coffee in cardboard cups, and the checker board was set up. "Red or black?" she asked.

"Black—like my coffee." He settled into his chair and took a cautious sip. "Ah. Perfect. At least they have decent coffee here."

Cheryl took a drink and set her cup down. "Too bad about the weather. We won't get nearly as much done as we'd hoped."

"I know. But we can't reschedule, so there's nothing to do but tough it out."

"Well, I've made out a dozen postcards, caught up with my journal, and read every magazine in this lobby."

He laughed. "You're doing better than me. I've just paced and fumed all morning, I'm afraid."

"I've been praying that God will move this storm out."

"Me, too. Maybe we could pray together?"

"I'd like that. Sometimes just hearing another person's voice makes me feel better." She held out her hand without hesitation.

He grasped it and bowed his head. "Lord, thank You for bringing us here safely. Now, if it pleases You, we'd like a chance to carry out the work we came to do."

"Heavenly Father," Cheryl said softly, "we know You're in control. Give us what's best. We hope that's clear weather. And thank You."

They smiled at each other. Cheryl opened her mouth then closed it abruptly.

"What?" he asked.

"Nothing. Well, I was going to say something, but I decided it was better not to. I feel better, since we prayed about this situation."

"It's been pretty frustrating."

"Yes. To be honest, I started wondering if I'd made a mistake in coming."

"Oh, please don't feel that way. I'm so glad you're here to keep me company. I can only take so much talk about mineral findings and ice core samples."

Her eyes picked up the gleam of the overhead light in the main part of the room. "I'm happy to be here with you, Ozzy. I just hope we're able to get out there and do the work, and that I'll live up to your expectations."

Oz looked toward the window, but the snow still swirled thickly. "Maybe it will clear off and we can go out tomorrow. We'll have plenty of snow for the snowmobiles to run in, but it might make it harder to spot the bears."

Grant Aron entered the lobby and looked around. When he spotted them, he walked quickly across the room. "Glad I found you. Nick just talked to the helicopter people. They said this is supposed to blow out tonight, and they can take out our supplies and equipment, except the snow machines, at first light. They said if we can run the snow machines out, it will simplify matters. They can take everything else in one trip. If they fly the snow machines, that will mean two extra trips, because they're so heavy."

"Well, it would save us a ton of money to do that, but it's forty miles."

"We can get there easily in a couple of hours, and they'll leave us extra gas for the machines."

"I don't know." Oz looked over at Cheryl. "What do you think?"

Her mouth had tightened, and her eyes contracted. "I. . .

whatever you fellows think."

"Did you ask Annette?" Oz asked.

"She's game."

Oz nodded. "Okay, we'll talk about it."

"All right. I'll see you in the dining room later. No one's going out for lunch in this storm."

Grant walked away, and Oz turned back to face Cheryl. "You're not thrilled with this development."

"Actually, it's a toss-up for me. A half hour in a helicopter or two on a snow machine. And you know what? I think the ground transportation is winning. We wear extra socks, that's all."

"Okay." He studied her face. "Does flying bother you? I noticed on the plane coming up here you seemed a little on edge. Have you flown much?"

"Not really, and not for a long time."

"It's very safe."

She grimaced and picked up her coffee cup.

"Why do I get the feeling I'm missing something? This isn't the first time."

She sighed and set the cup down. After staring at the checker board for a moment, she licked her lips. "Okay. I'm guessing Rick's never told you how my husband died."

Oz's heart clenched and he caught his breath. "Oh."

"Yes."

"Helicopter?"

"No, a small plane. In Puget Sound." She waved her hand in the air above the checkers. "I'm not afraid of flying. Not much anyway."

"It's when other people fly that it scares you. I can see why." He reached back in his memory, putting together the pieces. "That's why you weren't enthusiastic about my flying lessons."

Her face crumpled. "I'm so sorry. I tried not to show it. The last thing I wanted to do was put a damper on your fun. You've enjoyed it so much!"

He left his chair and stood beside her, sliding his arm around her. "Cheryl, sweetheart, you have no reason to be sorry. Forgive me for being so oblivious to your pain."

She shook her head, but tears streamed down her cheeks. She fumbled in the pocket of her zippered sweatshirt and came out with a tissue. "Really, I'm glad you like doing it. Having a pilot's license will be a huge help to you. You can fly to patients who live far out in the bush, and if you want, you can fly to your research areas next year. You could even join the Iditarod Air Force."

"I might just do that. But I'd hate to think you'd be worrying while I did those things."

She huffed out a laugh that was more of a sob. "I won't. I promise. God is going to help me get past this."

"I'm glad. But it will probably never go away completely. I mean, every time I hear about an officer killed on duty, I get a little depressed, remembering what happened to Jo. It's part of our nature."

"Yes, but. . ." She wiped her face and smiled up at him. "I truly believe I can work through this and get to a place where I let the Lord handle it. I can't protect you—or my kids or anyone else—by stewing about it. So I'll leave it to Someone who can."

He bent a few more inches and brushed her lips with his.

She kissed him back, and his pulse picked up.

"That's the way to look at it," he whispered. "Thank you." He sat down again opposite her.

Her eyelashes were still dark from her tears, but her eyes glistened, and her cheeks were flushed a becoming pink.

"Okay," he said, "now I'm going to trounce you at checkers."

"Ha. That's what you think."

eleven

The ringing phone on the nightstand woke Cheryl, and she groped for it in the darkness. "Yeah? Uh. . ." She tried to recall her room number.

"It's me, Ozzy. The weather's changed. The storm blew out to sea, and half the snow was swept away with it. How soon can you be ready to go?"

An hour later, all six team members had eaten breakfast and were ready to ride to the airfield, where their supplies were being loaded into the helicopter.

"I was hoping it would be a little warmer by now," Grant said, "but we'll take what we can get. We have a heater for each tent. Annette and Cheryl, your tent is smaller, so it won't take long to heat it. Just be sure you ventilate well. We'll only be forty miles from town, and if anything happens, we can call for the helicopter. We've got two satellite phones. I hoped for three, but they're expensive. We'd have had to give up some equipment for that. So we'll share. And Charlie has promised to keep his phone line open and come if we need him."

"So, we're all going on snowmobiles?" Annette Striker asked. She was closer to Robyn's age than Cheryl's, and her long, dark hair and flawless, olive-toned skin gave her an exotic air.

"We'll see what Charlie says," Grant told her. "I've got a rental outside. Ladies and gentlemen, if you're ready. . ." He gestured toward the door and they trooped out.

The men stood back to allow the women to climb first into a decade-old minivan. Cheryl took one of the middle seats. Annette opened the front door and appropriated the passenger seat. Cheryl was mildly surprised when one of the other men, Michael

Torrence, sat down next to her. Oz ended up in the back with the last of the geologists, Nick Weiss, and Grant drove.

Cheryl tried to follow the disjointed conversation. She'd learned all their names during their enforced stay in Barrow, but she was still sorting out their specialties and pet projects. Grant had taken leadership, ordered supplies, and organized their transport, but he had assured them all he was in no way to be considered the boss.

Nick, a graduate student in geology, would serve as Grant's assistant. He was the only one besides Cheryl who didn't have a Ph.D.

She'd begun calling the others "doctor," but Michael, a tall, blond man with a New England accent, had quickly put a stop to that. "We'll all work and live closely on this project. Let's stay with first names, if that's okay."

She didn't mind. It kept her from remembering every second that her higher education had ended after one year. She reminded herself that Oz had not chosen her because of her academic credentials but for her practical good sense and her work ethic. And he'd said they worked well together. That thought made her smile.

They reached the airfield in a predawn grayness at 7 a.m.

Their pilot, Charlie, was overseeing the loading of the last crates of gear onto the big helicopter. He waved them over and grinned. With his beard and fur-trimmed hood, it was hard to see his face, other than those gleaming white teeth. "Well, we finally got some flying weather."

"Is the chopper full?" Annette asked.

"We've got a little leeway." Charlie looked her up and down. "I can probably take two passengers. You want to fly?"

"Yes, please."

"Anyone else?" Charlie waved toward the three snow machines parked on the snowy tarmac to one side. "There's the transportation for the rest of you. Now, I can fly the machines out, if you want me to, but like I told Doc Aron, it will cost a lot more, and it will take more time in the long run."

"No, we'll be fine," Grant assured him. He looked at Cheryl. "Would you prefer to go in the chopper with Annette?"

She glanced at Oz, but he only arched an eyebrow. "No, thanks. I'd actually rather stay on the ground, if no one minds."

"I'll go in the chopper then," Nick said in his soft Kentucky tones. "Maybe Annette and I can get the small tent up before you get there, so you'll have a place to thaw out."

Grant chuckled. "You're just saying that because you never drove a snow machine before."

"Guilty." Nick winced. "I'm sure I'll learn quickly though."

"All right, let's load up and go," Grant said. "Cheryl. . ."

"She can ride with me," Oz said quickly.

She let out her breath, relieved that she wouldn't share a sled with one of the other men. Everything seemed new and a little scary.

Oz hesitated when they reached their snow machine. "Uh. . . I feel I should ask if you want to drive. You've put a lot more miles on snowmobiles than I have."

She smiled. "Thanks, but if it's all the same to you, I think I'll crouch behind you and let you take the wind in your teeth."

"If you're sure. . ."

"I'm sure. Besides, this way if something goes wrong, it'll be your fault, not mine."

He laughed. "All right then, m'lady, shall we embark?"

"You get on first."

He climbed aboard, and she straddled the seat behind him. She pulled her knit mask down over her face and peered out the eyeholes.

A few moments later, they were off, following Grant as he headed away from the airfield and out onto the open tundra. Michael followed on the third machine.

Cheryl hung on and enjoyed the scenery. In all her years in

Alaska, she'd never traveled above the Arctic Circle. The rising sun dazzled her, sending rays of gold, peach, and orange over the drifted snow. She looked back and saw the helicopter rise and head toward them.

Oz guided their snow machine over ridges of crusty snow and across innumerable frozen ponds. He avoided the drifts and rough places whenever possible, but sometimes the machine thwacked down over an uneven patch.

She squeezed the handholds to keep her weight centered. When the terrain smoothed out again, she let go and flexed her hands. Her insulated boots and gloves kept her warm.

Long before they reached base camp, she tired of the ride. She'd have sore muscles in the morning from all the bumps they rocketed over without warning.

Several times Grant slowed to check his bearings then roared onward. They'd been out an hour when the helicopter flew back over them. Charlie hovered for a moment and waved, then sped for Barrow.

Cheryl began to regret not taking the shorter ride with Annette. Of course, Annette and Nick now had the joy of setting up tents in the snow. *I'm just as happy to be right where I am, Lord. And thank You.*

Ozzie's solid bulk broke the ever-present Arctic wind, and she appreciated her sheltered seat behind him. Now and then he looked over his shoulder at her. She always gave him a thumbs-up or a nod so he'd know she was okay.

After the first hour, icicles formed on his beard where it poked out beneath the mask portion of his knit hat. She wondered if his toes were cold. Her own remained toasty, but she wished she could stretch her legs.

At last Oz turned and pointed with exaggeration ahead of them.

She craned her neck to see over his shoulder. A small black hump had appeared on the horizon. "Is that the camp?" she yelled in his ear, over the drone of the engine.

He nodded vigorously.

Cheryl realized her hands rested on his shoulders. He leaned back against her for a moment. She tightened her grip in a quick squeeze before she settled back and grasped the handholds again.

Annette and Nick had set up the small tent for the two women. They had also put several crates of supplies inside. When the snow machines halted nearby, both were struggling to lay out the larger tent. Michael and Grant hurried to help them.

Cheryl jumped off the machine and staggered as she found her footing.

Oz swung his leg over and stood. He gave a little groan and flexed his knees, with his hands pressed to the small of his back. "Man, I'm getting too old for this."

"Don't say that. It's our first day out." Cheryl turned her back to the wind.

"I know. I know." He chuckled and flipped his hood down, then pulled off the mask. "Whew. Feels good not to be pushing into the wind."

"I'm sorry. I should have driven for a while." She eyed him carefully, looking for signs of fatigue.

"I'm fine. But maybe you can find some coffee in all this organized chaos?"

Cheryl smiled. If one thing could make Oz feel at home out here in the snowy wilderness, it was a cup of hot, black coffee. She trudged over to where Annette was stretching out a tent flap.

"Hi. I don't suppose you and Nick spotted the coffee? I could start a pot."

"Fantastic. It's in our tent, beside the camp stove. I didn't have time to set that up yet."

"I'll get it." All those summers camping on the Kenai Peninsula with Dan and the kids would pay off handsomely now.

Cheryl hurried to the smaller shelter and ducked inside. In the semi-darkness, she almost stumbled over the small heater. The interior was passably warm. She peeled off her gloves and threw them on the farther of the two cots. A small duffel bag lay on the nearer one, and she assumed that was Annette's way of marking her territory.

The camp stove, nearly identical to the one they had at home, looked like an old friend. She lugged it outside and commandeered a wooden crate to set it on.

"Here you go." She looked up. Nick stood nearby holding a metal rack. "It's the stand for the stove."

"Wonderful. I'll have some coffee for you guys in no time."

"Sounds good."

By the time she'd found and filled the coffeepot and set it on the burner, they had the larger tent up and were lugging the rest of the gear into it.

Oz turned her way and brought her dark green duffel over. "This is yours, right?"

"Yes, thank you." She reached for it, but he shook his head.

"I'll take it in for you."

"Thanks. The second bed."

He returned in a moment while she rummaged in a box of dishes for mugs.

"So, what do you think?" His vivid blue eyes sparkled.

"So far, I like it. Are we going bear hunting today?"

"Thought we might, after lunch."

Lunch, she thought. Were the women expected to do the cooking? Maybe she would have to do it, because she was the least educated and didn't have a scientific mission of her own.

"Hey, Cheryl," Michael called, "I've got a crate of canned stew here. How about I open a couple of cans and put it on the stove? Can you get the other burner going?"

She nodded, feeling a sudden liking for the lanky, blond man. An hour later they had eaten, and Cheryl felt an eagerness to get on with the mission. The men pitched in to clean up and bear-proof the camp as much as possible.

Oz carefully selected the limited gear they could take with them on the snow machine. Cheryl put on a clean T-shirt and socks, in case those she'd worn all morning had absorbed sweat. She wanted to stay warm on this adventure, and she was determined not to complain if it killed her. When she went outside again, the wind had fallen, and the sun's rays now warmed her enough that she flipped her hood back and shoved her mask hat into her pocket.

Oz had a radio receiver sitting on the hood of the snow machine and wore earphones connected to the radio. He turned and smiled at her, but she couldn't see his eyes behind his sunglasses. "This is great. I'm picking up a fairly strong signal from a collared bear."

"We're not going out on the ice sheet, are we?" She glanced northward, toward Smith Bay and the Beaufort Sea.

"No, most of the bear population should still be on the land-fast ice or haunting the leads that have opened up near it. As the weather warms, the ice pack will move out from shore, but for now, most bears are sticking close to land because that's where the seals are."

She nodded. "Great. I've got my charts, notebook, and survival pack. Anything else I should bring?"

He reached out with his glove and touched her cheek. "I know the sun feels pretty good right now, but have you got your hat? It's bound to feel chilly when we start moving."

She patted her pocket. "Yes, sir, my cold-weather gear is all in order."

"Great. I've gone over the list, and I think we're all set. They're letting us take one sat phone today, since they plan to stick together on their first run. Let me just stow the radio." He put the receiver in a box of equipment on the back of the sled and climbed aboard.

Cheryl took her place behind him.

Nick and Grant had already started on their machine, with Nick in the driver's seat. He appeared to be taking a crash course in snow-sled driving from Grant. Michael waited near the third one for Annette to emerge from her tent.

Cheryl waved to him.

Michael returned her salute. "Good luck, and stay on the good side of those bears!"

Oz started the engine and put it in gear. Cheryl rather daringly rested her hands gently on his back for the first half mile. They came to a rough incline taking them closer to the coastline, and she reverted to clutching the metal handgrips provided.

What would the kids say if they could see her now? She looked toward the frozen sea, with the sun glittering on the drifted snow. Ridges of broken snow and ice littered their path, making the ride bumpy and uncomfortable again.

Oz stopped after about thirty minutes and let the machine idle while he got out the radio receiver. He put on earphones, and he grinned at her. "We're close. The signal's louder."

Cheryl looked around. "So there's a bear loose around here someplace?" All she could see was the rough snowfields and the ice sheet that covered the bay. A hundred yards offshore, a dark strip showed where a lead was opening in the ice.

"Let's get up on top of that hummock." Oz pointed to his right. "Maybe we can spot him from there. But if it's a sow still denned up with her cubs, she'll be harder to find."

Cheryl hung on as the machine toiled up the slope. Would the noise wake groggy bears or annoy conscious ones? A sudden uneasiness grabbed her. What if the knoll they climbed was a den? Surely Oz could tell if it were. Her neck prickled. She looked from side to side and behind them. Would her first encounter with a polar bear be too close for safety?

twelve

Oz drove carefully, mindful of cottony spots that could be deep snowdrifts. He didn't want the snowmobile bogging down on them in bear country. The vastness of the tundra and the nearby ice shelf affected him more than it had when he worked from a helicopter.

He and Cheryl were down on the same level with the huge bears and could run across one without warning. Past experience had taught him all too well the fragility of life in this hostile environment. He hadn't told Cheryl about the graduate student they'd lost to an unexpected crack in the Siberian ice two years ago. He didn't intend to tell her either. But he would be extra careful since the woman he'd lost his heart to clung to the sled behind him.

He stopped the machine on top of a rough ridge of broken snow and ice. Cheryl stirred, and he felt the light pressure of her hands on his back.

"Are we getting off?" she asked.

"Let's take a good look around first and make sure we're alone."

She pulled her binoculars out from inside her thick parka and scanned the terrain to their left.

Oz looked ahead and to their right. "Okay," he said after a minute of silent watchfulness. "Let's see what the radio tells us."

She handed him the receiver.

"Southeast," he said. "Let's take it slow and easy. I think we're really close."

"At least we're downwind."

It pleased him that she'd thought of that. Polar bears had the best noses in the world. "Right. I'll stay on the flat as much as I can, but look for drifts and humps of snow where there could be a den."

He'd provided Cheryl with dozens of photos of bear dens to give her an idea of what they looked like. An undisturbed den might not give any more warning than a small breathing hole in deep snow. An abandoned den, however, would appear as a gaping hole or a snow cave, perhaps with claw marks around it. He turned to give the radio back to her.

"Look! There he is." Cheryl was staring off in the direction the beacon had indicated.

He whirled around and scanned the tundra. "Where?"

"Two o'clock."

Oz narrowed his search and focused on a patch of discolored snow. As he watched, it moved. "I see him. Big, isn't he?"

The bear lumbered toward the bay, on a course that would make him pass in front of the snowmobile about fifty yards away. Though the shaggy animal looked thin, he probably weighed close to a thousand pounds.

"Slow now," he said. "Hand me the dart gun."

He heard her quiet movements. A few seconds later, she slid the rifle forward.

He took it, never looking away from the bear. The large male continued his trek toward the bay. Oz sent up a silent prayer of gratitude.

"Is the heaviest dose loaded?" she asked.

"Yes, I put one in, just in case we needed it in a hurry." Oz put the gunstock to his shoulder and sighted in. He waited motionless for the bear to reach the point where his path would bring him closest to the snowmobile.

Cheryl kept still.

At last the moment came, and he fired.

The bear jumped and swiped at its shoulder with a massive paw.

Cheryl shifted a bit but said nothing.

Without moving, Oz said, "Five minutes or so. Pray he doesn't see us first." Their vulnerability struck him. If the bear should spot them and charge, he'd have to choose between making a run for it on the snowmobile—which he'd shut off—or pulling his pistol. And that probably wouldn't be enough to stop it.

"He's going on," Cheryl whispered.

The bear padded toward the ice, pausing every few steps to bat at its shoulder again and sniff the breeze. After shuffling fifty feet farther on its course, it lay down and rolled.

Oz laughed softly. "He didn't like that."

"Think the dose will put him out?"

"Oh yeah." He turned and smiled at her. "Patience, my dear."

"I can hardly wait." Her tone was anything but eager.

"Don't you want to see him up close?"

"Yes and no."

"Well, it makes sense to be cautious with a critter like this. But once they're out, they generally stay out while we do our work. Then we give them the antidote and back off. They come to within minutes. This drug is wonderful."

The bear staggered to his feet and plodded on a few more yards then weaved, his head bobbing.

"He's going down again."

"Oz?"

"Yeah?"

Cheryl held the binoculars over his shoulder. "I don't see a collar on that bear."

He froze for a moment, took the field glasses, and raised them. As he peered through them at the bear, he tried to re-member if he'd noticed anything when it was closer to them.

"I can't tell," he said as the bear sank to its knees and elbows. "You know they're white, so other bears won't notice them. We'll have to wait and see."

"But if that's not the one giving off the signal we heard. . ."

He nodded and gave the binoculars back to her. "Then there's another one close by. Probably a denned sow." He looked all around, just to be sure he hadn't overlooked anything obvious.

The bear he'd darted lifted its head one last time then sprawled gracefully with its chin on its paws.

"Let's move in." He handed Cheryl the dart gun and started the engine. After driving to within ten feet of the bear, he turned the machine toward camp, so they could make a quick getaway if needed. "Stay here while I check him."

Cheryl leaned back, and he climbed off. He approached the bear. As expected, it didn't move. Oz walked around it to see if it lay comfortably in the snow, with none of the legs folded beneath it. He prodded it gently with his foot. The bear slept on.

He waved to Cheryl and she hesitantly approached. "It's humungous."

"Yup. And you were right. No collar."

Her eyes widened and she looked around. "You have the pistol, right?"

"Yes, I do. Okay, we're going to take vital signs first. Pulse, respirations, and body temp." Oz performed the tests, and Cheryl wrote down the results, staying a respectful distance from the bear's teeth and claws. Next Oz measured its length and girth. "He's kind of skinny," he told Cheryl. "Estimated weight, nine hundred fifty pounds. But he'll fatten up soon."

Next, he fixed white, numbered tags in both the bear's ears. Cheryl recorded the number, which was the same on both ear tags. "We use white because other bears don't seem to notice them," he said as he fastened the second one. "They've tried colored ones, and the bears tried to groom them off each other, like they would a bug."

She smiled. "What next? The collar?"

"Yes. Could you hand it to me, please?" Oz checked the battery and read off the serial number, then fastened the collar in place. "There. Now the tattoo."

She got the instrument out for him. He tattooed the same number that was on the bear's ear tags on the inside of its upper lips.

"One more thing," Oz said.

She nodded soberly and handed him the plier-like extractor. While she wrote the tag number on a plastic bag, Oz folded the bear's lips back on the side and removed the tiny premolar from just behind the bear's left canine tooth.

"How old do you think he is?" she asked, holding out the bag to receive the tooth.

"I'm guessing over twenty. But don't ask me how he kept from being caught all this time. This area's been monitored for quite a while now."

They packed up the tools. Oz reloaded the dart gun and double-checked the list on Cheryl's clipboard. "Okay, start the engine, and I'll give him the antidote." He administered the injection and hurried to hop on behind her. "Gun it, babe!"

She drove full throttle to the top of the rise from which they'd watched the bear and turned the machine sideways so they could both see the groggy animal raise his head and look toward the noise of the snowmobile.

"What if he comes after us?" Cheryl asked over the sound of the idling engine.

"He won't. He'll head for the sea."

"Okay. I'm just saying. What if?"

Oz wrapped his arms around her and gave her a gentle squeeze. "Then you hightail it for camp. They can swim for a hundred miles, but they can't run very far. They overheat easily."

"Think we could outrun him with this?"

"We won't have to." Even so, Oz found himself a bit on edge as they waited.

The bear shoved himself to his feet at last and lumbered slowly away from them, toward the ice shelf.

"Told you so." Oz nestled in against her hair.

"Will the drug affect him? Seems like I read it won't."

"No, there don't seem to be any long-term effects. It's been well tested and used for several years now. Once in a great while, a bear gets too big a dose, and then you have to resuscitate them."

"Just what I want to do—CPR on a bear."

He smiled. "At least we don't do mouth-to-mouth on them. But I'm careful with my dosage. I've only had to resuscitate one twice, and both times it was when someone else did the medicating."

"What about the other bear? The one that we heard the signal from before?"

"Oh, yeah." He gritted his teeth. Already it felt like he'd had a long day. He looked up at the sun then at his watch. "I guess we've got about three hours of daylight left. Shouldn't waste it."

She reached over her shoulder and patted his cheek. "Come on, Doc. Science awaits us."

Cheryl drove slowly along, below the rougher ridges of the snowscape. Hard to believe she'd touched a living wild polar bear. Oz kept watch with the binoculars as they rode, but she tried to stay aware of the area ahead of them, beyond her immediate path.

"Could be it's a sow still in her den," he reminded her. His breath tickled her ear. The sun was westering, and the temperature had declined a few degrees, but she didn't want to put her hood up. She loved having him ride behind her and occasionally brush her hair or give her a little squeeze. So much for her early resolution to keep a professional relationship with him. By now she knew it was hopeless, and her heart belonged to Oz Thormond.

"Hold it," he said close to her ear.

She eased the snow machine to a stop and looked to him for direction. He pointed toward the sea. A hummock of snow with a yellowish cast lay about two hundred yards away. She squinted. The sun sent long, low rays over the tundra to add cream and gray highlights. The hummock wriggled.

The object of her scrutiny suddenly came into focus, and she caught her breath. "Oh! She's got cubs!"

"Three, if I'm not mistaken." Oz took the strap from around his neck and handed her the binoculars.

"Aw! They're adorable. Can we get closer?"

"We have to." He frowned. "There's not much cover between us and them. Mama might not like it. I need to dart her and then wait for the drug to take effect. She might get protective when we get within shooting range."

Cheryl looked around. "If we go back west a ways and get behind some of those ridges, maybe we can get around beyond her without her noticing. There seem to be more knolls and drifts over there."

"Okay. But if the going is too rough, don't take any risks with the machine. We don't want a breakdown this late in the day."

She nodded, confident she could get him within a hundred yards of the bears without completely breaking from cover.

The short trip was more arduous than she'd expected, with rougher going and occasional breaks and deep cracks in the snow that she had to maneuver around. By the time they reached her goal, she feared the sow would have moved out of range. Oz got off the machine and took the dart gun from the scabbard. She followed him up a heap of frozen snow chunks, and they peeked over the top.

The sow and her babies rolled together playfully in the loose snow below them, only seventy-five yards away.

"Perfect," Oz said. "I should let you drive all the time."

"Can't we watch them for a while? They're so cute!"

"We need to make sure we're done and back to camp before dark."

"Right."

He shouldered the rifle and took aim.

"Don't hit one of the babies," Cheryl said, touching his arm lightly.

"I'll wait for a clear shot of Mom."

The sow cuffed one of the cubs playfully then rolled onto her back to let the three little ones nurse.

"They must have just left the den," Oz said.

"Can we examine the mother without tranquilizing the babies?"

"No, they've got claws and teeth, too. Besides, we want to tag the cubs. Can't do that without putting them out."

"Okay. Give me the dosage, and I'll get the darts ready for you."

"They must not weigh more than twenty pounds each."

He told her what he needed, and she went back to the snow machine. He had clearly marked the different syringes so they would not make a mistake. She took three of the smallest.

When she got back to his position, he lowered the rifle and turned. "Got a good shot at her, in her hip. She barely twitched. Once she's out, we can get down closer and do the cubs. They're so tangled up in her fur and with each other that I don't want to try from here and miss one or hit one twice."

Ten minutes later, the mother bear slept peacefully on the snow while one of her triplets continued to nurse and the other two wrestled with each other on her belly.

"Think she's out?" Cheryl asked.

"I don't know. She didn't lift her head like they usually do before they crash."

"Oz, maybe you should get closer and make sure she's breathing." The idea that the mother bear might be in distress while they laughed at the antics of her cubs made her feel ill and guilty. The animal's comfort and well-being always came first to a scientist.

Oz rose and made his way down the rough slope, carrying

the dart gun, which he'd reloaded with the lower dose.

Cheryl hesitated then followed. If he needed to resuscitate that bear, he'd need help.

He was ten feet from the sow when she raised her massive head and blinked at him. Oz froze and raised one hand, the signal for Cheryl to stop. The cubs scurried around to stare and sniff at him. The mother bear moaned. Her left front paw lifted for a moment, in a casual wave, then plopped onto the snow. The bear lowered her head with a big sigh and lay still.

"Is she okay?" Cheryl hissed.

Oz stood motionless for another fifteen seconds. He turned, blowing out a deep breath, his eyes nearly closed. "She's good. Out cold now, but breathing steadily. Come on."

He quickly dosed the three cubs. While they recorded the mother's identification number, measured her, and tested the battery in her radio collar, they let the little ones waddle about.

One of the cubs crumpled to the ground leaning against Cheryl's boot.

"Oh, sweet!" She shot a glance at Oz. "Can I pick him up now?"

"Should be okay."

She sat down and cradled the cub on her lap. The second had collapsed beside his mother, and the third wobbled on his feet.

"I want one of these." She swept her cheek over his fur.

Oz laughed. "You know how cute those pups of Robyn's are in the spring, and how a year later they've turned into fierce, competitive canines?"

She nodded. "I know. They don't stay little and cute. I still want one."

"Hold on a sec." Oz fumbled in the pockets of his bulky jacket and took out the camera he used to photograph his "patients." He zoomed in on Cheryl and the cub and clicked away.

"Thanks," she called. "My kids wouldn't believe this otherwise. But will the mother get upset when her baby smells like a human?"

"I've never known them to reject the cubs after we handled them, but I did bring that little bottle of fish oil."

"Oh, right. I can put some of that on him, and she'll think he's dessert, right?"

"She'll groom him well, I'm sure. Okay, we don't have to take a tooth from Mama, because she gave at the last blood drive. Let's measure the little puffballs."

She rose and carried her new pet to him, and Oz quickly clamped the tags to the cub's ears. Reluctantly, Cheryl set the baby down and retrieved her clipboard so she could record the numbers. She held each cub in turn while Oz measured them, estimated their weight, tattooed their lips, and took blood samples.

"Okay, I'll give the little guys their antidotes first. Then I want you to get up the ridge while I dose Mama. I'll join you, and we'll watch the family wake up from their siestas and continue on their journey."

"Think they'll go on toward the sea tonight?"

He looked around, studying the terrain. The shadows spread long now. "I don't know. I'm thinking they're not far from the den, because we heard the signal for hours before we found them. They may have just come out for some recreation this afternoon, and she might take them back to the den for the night."

"I expect she'll be a little disoriented when she wakes up. I mean, they've lost an hour or more. The sun is lower. . ."

Oz nodded. "Let's watch until we're sure she's alert." He injected each cub with the antidote.

Cheryl stayed to pat them until they began to stretch and wriggle.

"Okay, off you go," Oz said. He stood over the mother, holding the syringe with her dose of antidote until Cheryl had carried the dart gun and medical case to the top of the ridge that hid the snow machine. She turned and waved, and he bent over the sow. A moment later he'd pocketed the syringe and loped toward her. He climbed the ridge and sank down beside her, panting. "Has she moved yet?"

"Nope."

They sat watching, with the lowering sun behind them. It colored the snow with magenta, peach, and mauve. The sow's fur gleamed orange as her cubs began to tug at her.

Oz slipped his arm around Cheryl's waist. "Nice family group."

"Yes." She smiled up at him. "Thank you so much for bringing me out here. I would never in a million years have come to Barrow if you hadn't asked me."

He smiled. "If my beard wasn't full of ice, I'd kiss you right now."

She didn't know what to say, but she dared to lean back against his shoulder. He lowered his head to rest on hers. "You'd better put your hood up. It'll drop to sub-zero fast once the sun's out of sight."

She flipped it up over her knit hat and snapped it in place. It felt good, and she realized then that her ears had been cold for some time.

"Mama's getting up," he said.

The mother bear pulled herself up on her front legs and looked all around. She leaned over to lick one of the cubs. A minute later, she staggered to all fours and edged the cubs eastward with her nose. They waddled along to a snowdrift and disappeared beyond it.

"So that's where their den is," Cheryl said.

"I think you're right. And we'd better head for ours."

thirteen

The next morning, all of the scientists rose well before dawn and were ready to leave the base camp by seven, as the sky lightened to the south and east. Nick and Grant headed their snowmobile northward to study the ice sheet. Oz insisted that they take one of the satellite phones, as they were the most likely to have a serious accident. Michael urged Oz and Cheryl to take the second one, since they'd be working with potentially dangerous animals. He and Annette took a southwestern path, toward a glacier where they would take specific geological samples for an oil company partially sponsoring their grant.

Oz meticulously checked over the medical supplies and safety equipment while Cheryl performed a checklist on the snow machine. None of the others seemed to think much about the possibility of mechanical failure, but it weighed heavily on her mind. She lifted the hood and checked all the fluids and connections.

"Making the Arctic safe for science?" Oz asked with a grin as he stowed the dart rifle.

"Somebody's got to."

He laughed. "You're right, and I appreciate it. You're probably the most experienced snowmobiler among us. Sometimes I tend to get lost in my mission and forget I'm also responsible for my own transportation and well-being on this trip. Usually someone else supplies and operates the helicopter or snowmobiles or a tracked vehicle. I'm just along for the ride until we spot a bear."

"Where are we going today?" she asked.

"I'd like to go inland a couple of miles and look for dens a little farther from the coast. The sow we caught yesterday was just emerging with her cubs, and there are bound to be dozens more at the same point in the maternity cycle. The more cubs we can catch, the better."

Cheryl opened the compact book of satellite maps they carried with them. "Okay, so this way?" She ran her finger in a direct southerly course from the camp.

"And maybe a little eastward as we go. Biologists who've tagged bears in this area in the last few years have concentrated more to the west of where we are. I'd like to collar some new bears and put lots of fresh DNA samples in the mix."

"Would you like me to drive? I'm short, and you can look over my head. You could use the time spotting bears and not having to watch out where you're going."

"I think that's a great idea. I'll admit, I thought about it before, but I didn't want to suggest it until you felt comfortable driving out here and realized what we're up against."

"Well, the terrain is rough in places."

Oz nodded and looked pensively toward the southeast. "Not to mention that it's randomly sprinkled with thousand-pound carnivores."

Cheryl smiled but had to disagree, in light of her recent studies. "Not so random. We both know there are places more likely than others as denning areas."

"True. But we could still run into some adult males heading for the sea ice anywhere on the North Slope. Hungry adult males."

"Yeah." She glanced toward the tent she'd shared with Annette the night before. "Hey, if you're almost ready, there's one more thing I need to do before we take off."

"What's that?"

"I left a pot of fresh coffee keeping warm over a low burner, so I could fill the thermos right before we go."

Oz's face melted into contentment. "I knew I picked the right assistant for this escapade."

Cheryl hurried to where they'd left the camp stove set up between the tents. She turned off the burner and filled the thermos, then closed the stove and collapsed the stand. No sense leaving it out where a heavy wind could grab it. She took the stove and stand into the tent. They'd cached all their food in locked metal containers and stowed them in a hole in a snow ridge fifty yards from the tents. If somehow bears got wind of the food, the team didn't want them ravaging the tents as well. Of course, there was no guarantee, and with no one left to defend the camp, anything could happen during their absence.

&

Oz hung on to the snowmobile and scanned continuously. He'd hoped it would be easier to spot bears on level ground than from the air. Many times he'd nearly missed them when searching from a helicopter because they blended so well with their surroundings. On the ground, they'd at least stick up higher than the tundra. But he and Cheryl had been out nearly two hours and had nothing to show for it.

He lowered the binoculars. They were hard on his eyes while the sun shone. Ordinarily, he'd wear his sunglasses now, but he couldn't use the field glasses effectively with them on. Instead, he got a magnified image of dazzling snow.

The panorama of a broken, white windswept plain made him feel small. They traveled through a rough area that was full of frozen ponds and pressure ridges of ice, but no mountains. He couldn't remember a more desolate landscape. They were driving into the wind now, and the icy blast on his face as they rode prompted him to unroll the knit mask he'd kept in his pocket and pull it over his head, then replace his hood. He leaned forward and rested his chin on the shoulder of Cheryl's parka. "Feel like some coffee?"

She slowed the snowmobile and stopped in the shelter of a drift. When she shut the engine off, the stillness settled over them like a heavy quilt.

"Wow. I wish there were such a thing as a Stealth snow-mobile."

She chuckled. "What do you think? We haven't seen a thing so far."

"Let me try the radio again and see if we pick up any signals." He fiddled with it while she opened the thermos and poured the cup half full of black coffee. As he adjusted the receiver's position, he picked up a faint blip. "Hmm. If that's one of our bears, it's a ways away."

"Can you get a directional?"

"Maybe."

She handed him the coffee, and he took an experimental sip then a longer draft. "Thanks. That hits the spot. Have some, if you can stand it black."

"Maybe just a little." She sipped it and grimaced. "Yeah. That's the way you like it, all right. You want a granola bar?"

"Wouldn't mind. It's cold out here."

"I'm feeling it more today than yesterday," she admitted.

"I think the temp's dropped since we left camp. You okay?"

"Yes, for now."

They sat down on the snowmobile's seat and ate the high-calorie snacks, sharing a second cup of coffee.

"Well, shall we see if we can catch up to this bruin?" he asked.

Cheryl shoved the wrappers into a carrying bag while he stowed the thermos. "Can't go home empty-handed."

As they set out again across the trackless wilderness, his protective streak nagged at him. He tried not to think of all the things that could happen to Cheryl out here, fifteen miles from their base camp. He took up the binoculars again and studied every hummock of snow between them and the horizon.

&

They returned to base camp as the last rays of sun disappeared.

Annette and Michael waved from the cooking area between the tents. "We were getting a little worried about you," Annette called.

Cheryl walked toward them, staggering a little as she regained her land legs. "It took us forever to find the first bear. We only did three today."

"Sorry. Maybe you'll have better luck tomorrow."

"Do I smell chili?" Oz asked.

"Yes, sir," Michael replied. "Put your gear away and warm up. It should be ready in ten minutes or so."

The six of them ate in the men's large tent, sitting on cots and camp stools. Both kerosene heaters hummed steadily. It took Cheryl's feet a good twenty minutes to feel thawed.

"How are you doing?" Oz asked her as he stood to go for seconds.

"All right now, but I don't think my feet have ever been so cold."

"Let me take a look," Annette offered. "We don't want to risk one of us getting frostbitten."

"It was frigid out there today," Grant said. "We took a reading of five below zero this afternoon."

"Should be getting warmer by now," Nick said. He huddled on his cot wearing several layers of sweaters and his parka.

Cheryl felt silly to have the other woman examine her feet. She wanted to insist that they wait until they got into the privacy of their own tent, but Annette knelt before her and began peeling back her wool socks.

"They're still pretty cold." She cupped her hands around Cheryl's bare foot. "How's your feeling?" She ran a nail over the arch.

"I think it's okay." Cheryl smiled. "Your hands feel really warm."

Annette began to massage her foot. "Let's make sure your circulation's doing its work. You guys should have come back earlier."

"I guess you're right. We both got kind of stubborn and didn't want to turn back until we felt like we'd done a day's work. We opened the hood after we got done with the last bear and put our hands and feet on the engine to get them warm."

Oz came back with his replenished plate. "I don't think we'll go so far tomorrow, at least not if it's this cold. And we'll try straight south. Maybe the terrain is better for denning in that direction."

Cheryl shifted on the cot—whose, she wasn't sure—and leaned back on her elbows. "Thanks so much, Annette. That foot actually feels as if it belongs to me again."

"I don't see any discolored patches on your skin. Let's get the other one." Annette replaced the sock on Cheryl's left foot and reached for her right.

"You don't have to."

"I know, but I want you to be comfortable tonight."

"Yeah," Michael said, "she doesn't want you lying awake with frozen tootsies so that you'll hear her when she snores."

"I don't snore!" Annette sat back on her heels and glared at him.

"Oops, my mistake. Must have been Oz."

Annette sniffed. "Even if I *did* snore, it would have been a genteel snore you wouldn't have been able to hear in this tent, especially since you had your heater going." She peered at Cheryl's foot in the light of the lantern then began to rub it vigorously. "I don't see anything that looks like frostbite."

"Good. I wore extra socks, too." Cheryl let her continue for a couple of minutes then straightened. "Thanks so much. That feels much better."

"Do you girls want to play cards tonight?" Grant asked. He'd played endless games of rummy with Nick and Michael in the enforced evenings at the hotel and had apparently brought his deck into the field with him.

"No thanks." Cheryl rose. "I'm bushed. I think I'll wash my dishes and go to bed." To her surprise, Michael had suggested they clean up after themselves and they rotate cooking and washing the pans. Nick and Grant had drawn the K.P. duty tonight. Cheryl stuck her feet into her boots and clumped over to where Nick had set up the dishwashing station. When her plate, fork, and cup were clean, she rinsed them with water from a steaming kettle, dried them, and put them away. She turned to find Oz standing behind her.

"You sure you're all right?" he asked softly.

"I'm sure, but my bed seems very attractive right now."

He nodded. "Okay. I'll see you in the morning. And I promise we won't stay out so long if it's as cold as it was today." He gave her arm a gentle squeeze. "Sleep tight."

❧

The next day, Oz rose in the darkness and began preparing coffee. When the pot simmered on the stove, he went to the cache for breakfast food. The locked coolers they'd buried kept canned goods from freezing as well as discouraged marauding wildlife.

As he approached camp with his arms full, Cheryl emerged from the women's tent, wearing a headlamp like the one Robyn and other mushers used at night on the trail with their dogsleds. She stood looking up at the sky for a long moment before switching it on. "Good morning." She hurried to help him.

"It's Sunday," he said.

"Yes. Will that make a difference in our routine?"

"Not much. We've got to use every good day we have. But I thought, since it's our turn to get breakfast ready, that we might be able to move things along this morning and maybe have time for worship before dawn. That way we don't have an excuse for setting out late."

"That sounds great. I'm glad you thought of it." She worked quickly, speaking only when needed.

Twenty minutes later, Michael joined them.

The coffee had perked, and they'd sliced canned ham and set out biscuits, cheese, and canned fruit on the folding table, with chocolate bars for the scientists to carry with them that day.

"You guys are the model of efficiency." Michael sliced open a biscuit and piled cheese and ham between the halves. "Annette and I may get off on time today."

"We're going to pray together, and maybe read a psalm, in the big tent before we go." Oz set a cup of coffee down on the table beside Michael's plate. "Anyone who wants to is welcome to join us."

"Thanks. Is it Sunday then?"

"That's right."

Michael shrugged. "I wouldn't mind, but I don't think Annette's much for church and prayer."

Annette came out of the women's tent, zipping her parka. "Another cold one, I suppose."

"Yes, and I'm wearing double socks again," Cheryl said. "I tried for triple, but that made my boots too tight."

"Well, take some of those instant hand warmers. There's a box of them somewhere."

"I put a few in our gear on the sled," Oz said. "We've got hot coffee ready, and all the breakfast sandwiches you can make and eat."

"Mmm. Coffee first." Annette took a mug from him. "Where's the sugar?"

While she doctored her coffee, the other two men joined them.

"Are you guys going out on the ice pack today?" Michael asked.

"Well, it's getting a little dicey. We'll have to see how it looks," Grant said. "The water's starting to open up between us and the offshore ice. Yesterday we went straight north, and the ice was still thick enough there. But if we're not certain about it, we won't take chances."

Michael nodded. "We're gaining an hour of sunlight a week up here this month. Things are bound to break up. Be careful."

"We will."

"Good. Well, since it's Sunday, Oz suggested a group prayer

before we leave. I figure it can't hurt."

"Fine with me." Grant grabbed a plate and began fixing his breakfast in the lantern light.

Annette frowned but said nothing as she sipped her coffee.

"Man, it's cold." Nick shivered and reached for the coffeepot. "I move we adjourn this feast inside. No sense freezing out here until we have to."

Oz looked over at Cheryl. Again he regretted the discomfort she must be feeling on this expedition. "Why don't you go in, Cheryl. Enjoy your food, and I'll clean up."

"No, I'll stay and help you."

Oz hesitated. He could make a stronger appeal, but he didn't want to embarrass her in front of the others. Better to just hustle them to get the food they wanted and then put away the leftovers quickly.

"Okay. Anyone want to finish up this ham? I'd like to cache the tins and leftovers. If you want anything else, now's the time."

The others quickly replenished their plates and mugs then moved toward the big tent.

"We've got cleanup," Annette called over her shoulder.

"I know, but I don't want to leave anything out that might draw bears, even while we're eating," Oz said.

Cheryl swiftly helped him gather all the trash. Oz dumped the coffee grounds into the trash bag.

"Okay, you get inside and eat. And keep warm. I'll be there in a sec." Before she could reply, he scooted for the cache. Michael and Annette might be ready to pull out by the time he returned. If so, he wouldn't take it personally.

When he returned and entered the tent, Cheryl sat on a stool with her Bible open. The other three men sat on the cots, still sipping coffee, and Annette flipped through a sheaf of papers while she finished her breakfast.

"I always think about God when I get this far out, away from civilization," Grant said.

"I've heard that before—what you read," Nick said to Cheryl.

She looked up at Oz and smiled. "I was just sharing with everybody how I feel when I go outside and see the sky just crammed with stars—like this morning. We're miles and miles from any artificial light. Before I put my headlamp on, it was so awe-inspiring. Stars beyond counting."

"'The heavens declare the glory of God,'" Oz said.

"Yeah, that's what she read." Nick grinned at him. "Didn't know you were such a literature buff, Oz."

"It's the Bible, not literature." Annette didn't look up from her reports, and her voice held a tinge of annoyance.

"The Bible is some of the finest literature ever written," Oz said, "but it's a lot more than that. I believe it's God's Word."

Annette jumped up and pulled on her jacket. "Michael, I'm going to start loading our gear." She hurried outside.

"Is it me?" Oz looked around at the others, arching his eyebrows.

"It's not you," Grant said. "It's religion in general."

"I didn't mean to offend anyone." Cheryl's voice had lost its confidence.

"Hey, no offense taken here," Michael said. "I usually attend church on Sunday, and I wouldn't mind if you or Oz wanted to offer a prayer for our safety before we all pull out."

"Sure," Nick said. "I don't have a problem with that."

Oz nodded. "Thanks. Let's pray then." He caught Cheryl's eye, and she nodded slightly. Oz bowed his head. "Dear Lord, we thank You for bringing us here and allowing us to see and study Your magnificent creation. Give us safety and success in our missions, and bring us all here again tonight. Amen."

The others rose and wished them luck before dispersing.

Oz smiled over at Cheryl.

"I got my Bible out, and Michael asked about it," she said. "I didn't mean to start reading before you came in."

"Not a problem. Ready to roll?"

"Yes." She jumped up. "Just let me put this back in Annette's and my tent."

An hour later, they found their first bear of the day, a creamy sow traveling with a smaller bear.

"That must be a two-year-old," Cheryl called over the sound of their engine as they watched the pair.

"Yes, she'll be running him off soon and starting a new family."

By noon, they'd finished with those two bears and also caught and examined a female with two new cubs. They stopped to eat lunch on a choppy area of the glittering plain, with mountains just visible far to the south.

"I think it's warming up," Oz noted as he removed his gloves so that he could easily open a sandwich bag.

"Me, too."

"Toes warm?"

"Toasty." She ate in silence for a few minutes then smiled at him. "Well, today's a good day so far."

"It sure is. Only half over, and we've caught five bears." He popped the last bite into his mouth.

"Want the other half of this?" She held out part of her ham sandwich.

"Maybe later. I thought I'd have a granola bar."

She tucked the rest of the sandwich into its plastic bag and slid it into the pocket of her coat. "What would make this your all-time best day?"

He stopped chewing and cocked his head to one side. All sorts of thoughts flew across his mind. "You know, it would be hard to top being out here with you. And catching bears, of course. This is already one of the best days ever."

"Really? I mean. . .better than zoo work?"

"Much."

"Better than. . .I don't know. . .Siberia?"

"You're joking, right? We almost starved to death on that trip, and the—" He stopped just in time. He didn't intend to ever tell Cheryl about the time the helicopter had crashed on a snowfield or the student's drowning. "The biologist I was working with got sick and spent half the trip fighting off the flu. And that's only half of it." The other half could remain unsaid. He bit into the granola bar so she couldn't ask him another question right away.

She chuckled and flipped her hood back. The Arctic sun rippled on her rich brown hair, streaking it with auburn highlights. "I'm glad you lived to tell about it and came to Alaska."

He swallowed. "So am I." His voice went husky on him, and her eyes flickered. Oz slid one glove off again and reached for her. He ran his fingers into her shiny hair. "Very glad."

He leaned toward her and kissed her gently. When he released her, she looked up at him for a long moment then dove into his embrace, snuggling against the front of his parka.

"Ozzy, thank you for choosing me to come with you."

He held her for a bit, wishing he could shed the parka. Oh well, the cold might actually be a benefit, forcing them to focus on anything but the physical in their relationship. He cleared his throat. "I've been thinking about it for a long time. About you and me, that is. I think I'm ready for—"

Movement in his peripheral vision grabbed his attention, and he stopped.

Cheryl must have felt his intake of breath. She pulled away from him. "What is it?"

"Easy. There's a huge bear about ten yards away from us."

fourteen

"Does he see us?" Cheryl asked.

"Oh yes."

Ever so slowly, she turned her head. To her credit, she didn't yelp or even gasp when she caught sight of the massive, yellow-white bear looming on a heap of crusty snow, staring at them. Her grasp on Oz's forearm tightened.

He shot up a barrage of prayer fragments. Which could he draw quickest—the pistol or the dart gun? If he darted the bear, it would take him ten or fifteen minutes to go down. And the pistol wouldn't stop a bear easily.

"Can you reach the keys? I'm thinking that if you started the engine, the noise might scare him off." Oz tried to keep eye contact with the bear, hoping it wouldn't notice her stealthy movement. "You can back this thing up, right?" He tried not to let even his lips move.

"Yes, but not very fast. So what do we do if he comes toward us when I start the engine? They say to wave your arms and yell."

"I don't think we can out-yell the snowmobile. I'll make a dive for the gun."

After a pause, she asked, without looking at him, "Which one?"

Oz gulped and sent up another prayer. "Dart rifle, I guess."

The big bear opened its mouth and yawned. The sound of a bored bear couldn't keep Oz from noticing its oversized canines.

"Okay, I'm touching the ignition." Cheryl's voice shook.

"Do it. Just don't move toward him. I'll go for the dart gun. You ready? On three. One, two, three. . ." He whipped around and pulled the rifle from the scabbard. He always kept it loaded

131

with the adult dose while they drove, but this bear must weigh twice what any of the females they'd caught did. Would he get a chance to reload?

The engine gurgled and roared to life. The bear reared on its hind feet and loomed impossibly big. Oz jerked the gunstock to his shoulder and fired. Cheryl eased the snowmobile back a few feet.

The bear let out a roar and clawed at its left shoulder, where the dart had landed. As the huge beast plummeted to all fours and down the snow heap, Cheryl stood suddenly and threw something. "Hang on!"

It took Oz a moment to realize she'd lobbed the half sandwich toward the bear. As the snowmobile zoomed forward, Oz rocked back in the seat, clutching the dart gun. They swept within ten feet of the bear as Cheryl cranked the tightest turn she could.

The bear jumped back but didn't run away. Maybe it was curious about that ham sandwich. Oz stared at the bear, mentally cataloging the shape of its head and the odd color of its legs.

Cheryl squeezed the throttle, and they roared farther away in a big arc.

Oz craned his neck to continue studying the bear for a few seconds. "He's not following," he yelled in her ear.

Cheryl backed off on the gas. The snowmobile slowed, and she turned it broadside so they could both look back without letting the machine face the bear. "Should we keep going? Or wait for him to go down?"

"The dose might not put him out. I was loaded for a sow at spring weight. That guy's got to weigh at least a thousand pounds. I'm guessing more."

"He's fatter than that first one we caught." Cheryl eyed the bear as it lumbered down off its perch and sniffed along the ground. "He's going for the sandwich. If you reload, we could go a little closer, until you're comfortable with the range, and you could hit him again."

"I don't know." Oz gritted his teeth, weighing the risk. "Right now we're far enough away that we could outrun him if he decides we're a sandwich machine. Remember, polar bears overheat really fast when they run."

She nodded. "So he couldn't chase us very far."

"Right. But I don't know *how* far. And if we go closer. . .he's got a taste of that ham now. I'm thinking it's too risky." All the reasons he preferred to stalk bears from a helicopter came back to him.

"But we've got to collar him! He's huge, Ozzy!"

"I know. And there's something else."

"What?" She turned and looked at him, her brow puckered in a frown.

"What color is he?"

"Cream? Yellowish, I guess. Hey! His legs look darker."

"Exactly. And did you catch a profile view?"

Cheryl caught her breath. "His head is wide, like a grizzly's."

"Exactly."

"Oh, Ozzy, come on! We can't not catch this guy. He's a grolar bear!"

&

Cheryl watched the bear shuffle along the snow, sniffing as though hoping for more sandwiches.

"I wonder if he ate the plastic bag. Oz, we have to put him down." She turned halfway around. "Get the gun ready. Come on! We can't miss this chance."

"Cheryl, sweetheart, calm down. Think about this. That is a carnivore we're talking about. The biggest land carnivore there is. And you want to ride right up close and pop him with a dart."

"We've caught three males since we started this project. What's one more?"

"I'll tell you. We saw the others before they saw us, and we sneaked up on them. This one has not only seen us, he knows we taste good, and we've annoyed him."

"But this machine can go fifty miles an hour. You said yourself we can outrun him. I know we can."

"If he's half grizzly, maybe not. He might not have the genetics that would make him overheat. Besides, we don't want him to overheat and maybe die of heart failure."

She sighed. "Okay. I'll do whatever you say."

"Aw, Cheryl." He shook his head and wrapped his left arm around her shoulders, giving her a squeeze. "I love you too much to be reckless with your life. Right now, we're far enough away. But if we drove in another hundred yards and he came at us. . ."

His passionate speech was lost on her after the first few words. "Did you say. . .you love me?"

He laughed. "Of course. You're a smart woman. You must have figured that out by now."

She shook her head. She'd hoped. She'd wondered. But hearing him confirm her suspicions brought her a wave of tenderness and joy she hadn't expected out here in the frozen wilderness. Even when Oz had kissed her at their lunch stop, she hadn't quite been able to convince herself they were heading for a permanent relationship. "I. . .I love you, too."

He smiled and looked back toward the bear. "We'll have to discuss that in detail later. Right now, I'd better reload."

The bear ambled toward them, almost as if he were out for a leisurely stroll.

"Do you think he's feeling groggy?" Cheryl asked.

"I hope so, but groggy isn't good enough." He slid the rifle's bolt shut. "Okay, listen. If you can make a big swing like you did before and come around on his flank, I'll try it. I'm counting on him feeling the effects of the first dose by now. But I don't want to get too close. If he heads toward us, so I can't get a good shot, you get us out of there."

"Got it." She grinned at him. "Wait till Robyn hears."

Cheryl maneuvered the snowmobile slowly, so as to keep the engine puttering as quietly as possible.

Oz kept the dart gun aimed at the oddly colored bear, wondering how many kinds of fool he was. This shot should have been made from a hundred feet in the air above the bear, where there was no chance it could get at them, no matter whether the dart hit squarely or the dose was figured correctly.

The bear paused and turned, watching them as they circled, marking time but always facing them. The big bear seemed determined not to expose his sides for a clean shot into either shoulder or hip.

Oz held off, knowing each second he waited prolonged their danger. "Stop."

Cheryl obeyed immediately, bringing the machine to a halt.

"Keep your hand on the throttle. We may need to make a run for it." He glanced ahead. They had a clear path, should they need it.

The bear took a few steps toward them and paused to bite at his shoulder, worrying the spot where the first dart had hit him. Oz leaned his left elbow against Cheryl's shoulder to steady his aim.

"If I say go, you go, no matter what."

"I hear you." She sat perfectly still.

The bear rose on its hind feet and opened its cavernous mouth in a roar. Oz gritted his teeth and shoved down the impulse to flee. Once again, the mammoth bear twisted its head around to nip at its left shoulder, exposing the outside of its right foreleg and shoulder. Oz pulled the trigger. Again the beast roared. It dropped to a running position.

"Go!" Oz lowered the rifle and held on to the sled.

Looking back, he saw the bear run a few yards after them and stop. It turned its head and tried to reach the spot of the new injection.

Cheryl accelerated and they zoomed forward, over the rough snowfield, away from the bear.

When they'd gone a quarter mile, Oz tapped her shoulder. "Slow down and arc around where we can watch. He's not following."

She eased the snowmobile about. Oz could barely see their quarry now because of the choppy terrain.

"Should we go back?" she yelled.

"Let's give him ten minutes or so of peace. How's our fuel?"

"Good."

He nodded. "Keep the engine running." No use stressing the bear by approaching again and hoping the next charge would be another feint. He reloaded the dart gun and placed it in the scabbard then raised his binoculars. "I think it's just a matter of time now, but we need to be cautious. When he starts weaving, we'll go a little closer, but I don't want to upset him and ruin the advantage we have."

"Okay." Cheryl looked up at the sun then at her watch.

"We've got plenty of daylight," Oz said, and she nodded. It seemed hours had passed since he'd spotted the bear, but it was only two-thirty, and the sun would shine until almost seven.

"I know what you're thinking," Cheryl said.

"What's that?"

"That if we'd been in a chopper, we'd have had him easily, without the risk."

"There's some truth to that. But there are always risks. And honestly, in a helicopter, we might not have even seen him."

They waited in silence. The sun beat down, and Oz unzipped his parka. Spring was coming to the North Slope, no question.

"I guess the bay will be mostly open when we leave," Cheryl said.

"Probably. Grant said he didn't know if they could get out on the pack ice safely anymore."

"I hope they stayed on the land-fast ice today."

"Yeah, it's turned out pretty warm."

Cheryl stood on the machine's running boards. "Hey, can you see the bear?"

Oz rose and focused the binoculars. "I see him. I think he's down, but there are a lot of ridges between us. Let's go a little closer."

He sat down, and Cheryl drove slowly. When the bear was clearly visible, Oz clapped her shoulder. "Stop here."

The animal sat on the snow, licking its shoulder. It raised its head and looked toward them then lumbered to its feet.

Oz caught his breath. Had he made another mistake and approached too soon? A hundred yards of tundra still separated them, but they were pointed directly toward the bear again.

Cheryl turned halfway around on the seat. "He's staggering."

"Yup. Keep ready anyway."

The bear plopped down again and rolled over, batting at the air, then settled with its chin on its front paws. Just when it seemed quiet, it raised its head and stared at them.

"He's going out." Oz grinned in satisfaction. That final lifting of the head was a classic sign that the drug had done its work.

Gently the bear lowered his jaw again and rested. Its eyes closed.

"Yay!" Cheryl turned and raised her hand for a high-five.

Oz complied, laughing. "Let me approach him first, just in case, but if I ever saw an unconscious bear, that's one right over there."

He got off the sled and took the dart gun, walking swiftly but with caution across the snow. Ten feet from the fallen animal, he stopped, overwhelmed by what they'd done.

The bear was huge, maybe the biggest one he'd ever caught. Even in the lean springtime, it must run more than twelve hundred pounds. Its fur morphed from creamy on its back and shoulders to yellow on its sides. Its lower legs were a mottled brown, and brown hairs also circled its muzzle. Instead of the elongated skull of most polar bears, its head was broader and its face flatter.

He stepped closer and prodded the bruin with the muzzle of the rifle. It continued its peaceful slumber. Oz exhaled and closed his eyes for a moment. "Thank You, Lord. I don't deserve this."

He turned and beckoned to Cheryl. She puttered in slowly and parked the snowmobile five yards from the bear, pointed toward camp.

Together they unpacked their equipment. "You think it's a real grolar?" she asked eagerly.

"I do, but the DNA we get now will be the proof. Take the camera and start getting pictures. This is historic."

Other hybrid grizzly-polar bears had been documented. The different types of bears were known to breed, both in zoos and in the wild. A hunter had killed one a couple of years ago, thinking it was all polar bear, and discovered after the bear died that it was part grizzly. But no one had ever examined, tagged, and collared a living grolar bear in the wild.

Scientists would have a heyday, tracking this fellow to see where he chose to wander. Would he take to the pack ice this summer, to hunt seals? Or would he stay ashore and favor the grizzly's diet of vegetation and fish? A million other questions came to Oz's mind as he worked.

Cheryl photographed the bear from every conceivable angle and clicked more photos to document Oz's work.

He measured the skull and girth meticulously and took several vials of blood. He removed the premolar tooth, which seemed large for a polar bear. Before putting the collar on, he tested it to be sure it would work correctly. "I've got to adjust this to the largest setting. This guy's neck is huge."

"All of him is huge." Cheryl brought him the ear tags. "I wish we could stay and follow him around."

"Yeah. I think he's around four or five years old." Oz touched a scar on the bear's face. "He's had at least one serious fight."

"This is so exciting. If he mates and has offspring. . ."

"Yeah. With the DNA, we'll be able to match it to his cubs,

if there are any." Oz shook his head, still realizing what he was doing.

"Should we call someone outside on the satellite phone?" Cheryl asked. "How big is this?"

He paused with the ear tags in his hand. "I don't know. They're not going to come get him and put him in a zoo. At least, I don't think they would. I hope not. But collaring and tagging him will give us a chance to follow him for years. That's major. In fact. . ." He grinned at her. "In fact, the article we publish this summer will probably get us a grant to come back here next spring."

"We? Us?"

"Absolutely. I couldn't have done this alone. In fact, if you hadn't been driving, I'd probably have flooded the engine I was so excited, and right now I'd be the entrée he chased down your sandwich with. I expect you to help write the paper. And do the interviews with me."

"What interviews?" she asked.

"Listen to you. We can be on the Anchorage news next week, if we want, and it will escalate from there. Newspapers, magazines. . ."

"If we want?"

"Well, yeah. We have to decide whether we want to publicize this immediately or wait until we've analyzed all the data and written our scientific papers and our new grant proposal." The idea of continuing to work with Cheryl held a definite appeal. He could see himself working with her for a long time to come.

"Is there an advantage to waiting?" She glanced down at the bear. "Don't answer that now. We need to finish here and get this guy back on his feet."

"Right." Oz went back to work. He examined the claws, teeth, and other features that might exhibit a peculiarity of either the grizzly or the polar bear. When they'd done all the standard testing, sampling, and tattooing, he stood back. "It's funny, but I hate to leave him."

Cheryl nodded, watching the big animal's side rise and fall. "I know what you mean. This is special. Once he's awake and we leave, this part will be over. We may never see another grolar."

"Or is it a pizzly?" Oz chuckled at her widened eyes. "That's what they call hybrids with a polar bear father and a grizzly mother. A grolar is the other way around. Well, time to pack up the equipment, I guess."

Cheryl looked over her checklist. "I don't think we've forgotten anything."

"Just a picture of you with Gargantua." Oz reached for the camera and took several pictures of Cheryl next to the big bear.

They packed everything securely on the snowmobile, and Cheryl started the engine.

Oz injected the bear with the antidote and climbed on behind her. "Let's go."

She drove a safe distance away, and they watched until the bear pushed to its feet and walked unsteadily away, toward the northeast. Oz's slight sadness at seeing the magnificent animal leave them was tempered by the latent excitement he felt at the thought of finding this bear's cubs another year.

They arrived at the base camp just as the sun was setting, washing the snow with swaths of fuchsia and salmon. Cheryl parked the snowmobile and turned off the engine.

An unnatural silence lay over the camp. The other two snowmobiles were not in sight. No one had set up for supper. The tents stood dark and empty before them.

Cheryl twisted around and looked at him. "They're not back yet."

fifteen

Just to be sure, they checked both tents, but they were alone in camp. Cheryl met Oz outside, where they usually cooked.

"It's early yet," Oz said, but she couldn't stop the adrenaline that surged through her.

"Should we try to call them?"

"Yeah, why don't you try to raise them on the sat phone while I put away our gear."

He opened the box on the back of the snow machine, and she seized the phone.

"Take it in your tent, and I'll come get your heater going in there," Oz said.

She hurried inside and sat down on the edge of her cot. She fumbled for her headlamp and put it on so she could see to make the call.

Oz came in with the box that held most of their traveling supplies and set it on the floor. He lit the lantern first then the heater.

Cheryl's hands trembled as much from tension as from the extreme cold. She punched the numbers in wrong on her first try and had to start over. Finally she got it right. She stared across the tent at Oz, where he still knelt by the heater, listening. "No one's responding."

"That's odd. Try again?"

She severed the connection and held out the phone. "You try, please. I'm shaking so badly, I don't know if I can do it again."

He came over, took it from her hand, and laid it on the cot. He grabbed a wool blanket off Annette's cot and wrapped it around Cheryl's shoulders. "Get over by the heater. As soon as we make contact, we'll get some coffee heating."

She nodded and stepped over near the faithful heater, which glowed a comforting orange. She unzipped her parka but kept the blanket draped over her shoulders while Oz tried to call the geologists.

After a minute of silence, he pushed more buttons. "Yeah, Charlie? This is Dr. Thormond, with the scientific team."

Cheryl whipped around and stared at him. She hadn't really expected him to call in the cavalry so soon, but Oz was taking this as seriously as she did.

"Yeah, my team was a little late getting back to camp tonight, and we expected the other four to be here when we arrived, but it's deserted. Yeah. . . Uh-huh. . . Okay, I guess that makes sense." He signed off and laid the phone down.

"What did he say?" Cheryl asked.

Oz walked over and laid his hand on her shoulder. "He says to give them time to get back or at least call us. And if they're not here by dawn, he'll fly out here."

"Dawn? That's twelve hours."

He checked his watch. "Less than eleven, actually, but yes. Charlie can't search effectively in the dark, not knowing where they are."

Her lower lip trembled, and she clamped her mouth shut. Oz drew her into his arms. She clung to him, sliding her hands in under his open parka and pulling close to his solid, comforting warmth.

He patted her back rhythmically, through the layers of down, wool, and nylon. "Let's pray."

She nodded, her head moving against his chest. "Yes, please."

Oz let out a long sigh. After a moment, he said softly, "Heavenly Father, we're at a loss. Show us what to do. Please protect the others. We don't know what's delayed them, but it can't be good." After a few seconds of silence, he straightened. "I think

I should go look for them."

Cheryl caught her breath. "That would be too dangerous. We don't know where they went. Shouldn't we stay in camp until daylight?"

"Ten hours is more than enough time for unsheltered people to freeze."

"I. . .I just don't know." Fingers of fear clawed at her stomach. "Do you think they're together? I thought they had separate plans."

"They did, but they may have stuck together, especially if Grant decided they couldn't go out on the icepack safely. He and Nick may have opted to tag along with Michael and Annette and run their experiments onshore."

"May have."

"The odds are good that they're together, or at least one team would have come back on time."

She didn't like that but couldn't think of an argument. "Why aren't they answering the phone?"

"I don't know. Maybe the battery died. Cold can do those things in."

"Yes, but we're all careful to keep the phones insulated."

Oz sighed. "I wish I had answers for you. But I think Michael and Annette were going to follow the coast east. Grant and Nick may have gone that way, too, looking for good, solid ice where they could get offshore. I can look for tracks."

"I'll go with you."

"No, you need to stay here. I'll take our phone. If they come back, you can use their phone to call me. And if their battery is dead, we have an extra one in our tent."

"But, Ozzy—" She gulped. It wasn't that she was afraid to stay alone. She'd done that many times. But to be alone for hours, wondering if he was safe. . . It would be too much like the night she'd waited for news of Dan. She remembered when she got the devastating news and learned of the men who'd gone out to help her husband and lost their own lives. Tears formed in her eyes, and a painful lump grew in her throat.

"What, sweetheart?" He stroked her cheek and tilted her chin up.

"I don't know if I can do it. Wait for you, I mean. And not know you're safe."

He pulled her close and held her tightly for a long moment. "Cheryl, I don't know what else to do, and I can't do nothing."

She sniffed and pulled away, brushing at her overflowing tears. "All right. I understand."

He eyed her carefully. "We have flares." She nodded. They always took a couple in their emergency kits. "I'll take some more with me. I'll set one off if I find anything."

"Okay. I'll go outside every five minutes and look."

"Every fifteen."

"No, every ten."

He smiled gently. "All right. And I'll leave you a couple. If you have news and you don't have a phone, put up a flare. I should be able to see it for a good many miles."

"Okay, but you have to keep looking back."

"Don't worry, I will."

She bit her lip. The stress showed in his sober expression. The ice in his beard had melted, and it glistened damp in the lamplight.

"Cheryl, I love you. And I will come back." He drew her to him and kissed her tenderly.

She kissed him back, hoping he could decipher her fear and confusion and understand how much she loved him and the ache that came as she agreed to let him go.

He squeezed her and stepped away. "Pray, sweetheart. And I'll see you soon." He left the tent.

She sat down stiffly on the edge of her cot, too numb even to think a prayer yet. A few minutes later, the snow machine's engine roared to life.

⋙

She went outside into the bitter cold. Oz had been gone ten minutes. She peered toward the east. A reddish glow lit the sky. Her heart leaped, until she realized it was the aurora, putting on its ghostly show. Could she tell the difference if Oz set off a flare?

In her parka's pocket she'd stuffed a loaded flare gun and an instant hand warmer. She paced between the tents. He'd gone off without the promised coffee—without any supper either. She should have insisted he fortify himself before he left.

At least she could set up the stove and have hot coffee ready when he and the others came back. She hurried into the men's tent and got out the camp stove and stand. The dart rifle lay on Oz's cot. She paused, looking at it. Had he taken his pistol? He must have. She picked up the rifle and checked it. Loaded for bear. She smiled at that thought and shouldered it. At least she'd have a delayed-action weapon while she raided the food cache.

Another ten minutes must have passed. She studied the east carefully. The aurora still danced in soft pink and mauve ripples over the starry sky. Wispy clouds diffused the color into magenta and violet. Any other time she'd have marveled at the display. Tonight it was a distraction. . .maybe even a camouflage. She sought in vain for the starker, red-orange glow of a flare.

At last she turned her headlamp on and trotted toward the cache, holding the dart gun at the ready. The men had left a spade sticking in the snow near their hiding place and she quickly opened a hole and pulled out the first locked cooler. She'd forgotten to fetch the keys from the hook on the tent pole in the men's quarters.

She jogged back to get them, praying constantly and scanning the east, where the colorful sky met the snow-covered land. It was never truly dark here, unless a storm obliterated the night sky.

Once she had the keys, she headed back to the food,

walking this time and breathing hard. She needed to start a regular regimen of exercise once she got home, so she'd be in better shape next year when she and Oz came back to look for those grolar cubs.

A half hour later, she had a pot of coffee simmering. She'd heated a can of stew and forced herself to eat half of it. It wouldn't do to let her anxiety keep her from eating. She paced between the tents, swinging her arms and stomping her feet frequently, sending up a continual stream of prayers. Her hands and feet numbed. She turned toward the heated tent for a warming session. As she stood before the heater and dropped her gloves to the floor, the thought she'd tried to suppress attacked her head on.

What if Oz didn't come back?

sixteen

Cheryl had been alone in camp nearly two hours. She'd wept, and she'd dried her eyes so the tears wouldn't freeze on her cheeks when she went outside again. She'd lectured herself, and she'd cried out to God. If only Oz hadn't taken the sat phone with him, she could call Charlie in Barrow and demand that he send someone out immediately.

She pulled on her knit mask and gloves once more and shuffled outside, carefully closing the tent door so the heat wouldn't escape with her. She turned eastward. The aurora had faded, except for one spot, where it shone brighter than ever, far to the east and just a little south.

It took her a good half minute to make sense of what she saw and realize it was the light of a flare, reflected off the clouds. "Oh, thank You, thank You, thank You!"

She dashed to the food storage again and set about preparing plenty of nourishment for the entire team. She kept warm by cupping her gloved hands around the coffeepot and continued to stare eastward. Every few minutes she lowered her hood and pulled her hat up off her ears to listen, but she couldn't do that for long. In a frighteningly short time, her ears began to ache, and she covered them again.

At last she thought she heard an engine. She ran a few steps away from the stove, so its sputtering didn't mask other sounds. That was definitely a motor. Almost at once, a pinprick of light appeared in the distance. Five minutes later, a lone snow machine pulled into camp and stopped before the men's tent. She ran to it, rejoicing to see two riders and trying to identify them.

"Cheryl! Help me with Annette."

"Grant?"

"Yes." He held a hand up in front of his face as her head-lamp's beam caught him in the eyes.

"Sorry." She reached up and switched it off. "Is Annette hurt? And did you see Ozzy?"

"Yes, this is his snowmobile. Help me get Annette inside, and I'll tell you all about it."

Grant had left the machine, but Annette still huddled on the seat.

"Of course." Cheryl hastened to help him.

Annette moaned as they took her arms and raised her off the machine. "Are we there?"

"You're here," Cheryl said. "It's warm in our tent. Come on, honey, we'll get you inside, and I'll bring you something hot to eat."

She and Grant walked on either side of Annette, with Grant bearing most of her weight. Cheryl opened the tent door, and they half carried her through. While Grant lowered her onto her cot, Cheryl closed the door and moved the heater closer. Annette groaned as Grant lifted her legs onto the cot.

"It's going to be okay," he said. "We'll take your boots and things off. It's warm in here, Annette. You're going to be all right." He shot an anxious look at Cheryl.

"I'll get her things off," Cheryl said. "You get warm. You must be half numb yourself."

"I am. Be careful of her left side. She's pretty bruised up, but I don't think anything's broken."

Annette's bootlaces were frozen in clumps of ice. Cheryl struggled with them for a minute and then pulled a knife from her survival gear and cut them. She eased the boots off. The wool socks followed. Annette's feet felt like blocks of ice.

Cheryl looked over at Grant, who had shed his parka and squatted by the heater, extending his trembling hands toward it.

"Grant, this looks really bad. What should we do? Warm water? Massage?"

Grant came over and touched Annette's feet. "No discoloration. Try massage. I'll go to the other tent and bring the second heater over."

"No, you stay here. I'll get it." Cheryl hurried to the men's tent, which she hadn't bothered to heat. No sense wasting fuel to warm the larger area when no one was there to use it. She carried the heater to the women's tent and set it up so the two units would warm Annette's sleeping area from both sides.

"Can you check the fuel and light it?" she asked Grant. "I'm going out and get that coffee and stew I fixed for you. I think you need it."

"No, you need to go back for the others."

"It will take me two minutes, and I think it's important."

He gave in, and she ran to fetch the hot food and coffee.

"Thanks," he said when she returned. "I think Annette's sleeping naturally. She needs to see a doctor, but I think she'll be okay. She was a good scout."

"What happened?" Cheryl asked.

"Nick and I spent most of the day out on the pack ice. We headed back to camp, and shortly after we got to shore, we saw a flare go up, a little to the southeast. Of course we rushed over there. Michael and Annette's snowmobile had fallen down into an ice ravine, and they couldn't get it out. Annette had managed to set off the flare."

"Didn't you have the sat phone? We tried to call you."

Grant shook his head. "They had it, and their gear dumped when the machine went down. The whole snowmobile rolled over several times and bounced down that crevice. They lost the phone. Nick and I got Annette out, but it took us almost an hour to get Michael up out of the hole. It was dark by then, and we couldn't start our snowmobile."

"I'm so sorry. What can I do to help?"

"Oz said that if we got back here with the snowmobile, we could hitch up the cargo sled and take it back for Michael. He's hurt bad."

"Of course."

Grant shook his head. "You know, I thought that extra sled was a waste of money and space in the chopper, but I'm glad now we've got it. They're out there trying to keep everyone warm. We were wondering if Nick or I should try to walk back to camp for help when Ozzy showed up."

"I'll go right now." Cheryl pulled her mask hat on.

"Are you sure? I'm feeling lots better now."

"Absolutely sure. You stay here with Annette. The thermos Oz and I use is over there. Fill it with coffee for me. I think I can hitch up the cargo sled by myself. If I need help, I'll come get you."

"Okay." Grant sounded doubtful, but already Cheryl had her hood fastened and her gloves on again. She hurried outside and moved the snow machine to the side of the big tent, where they'd parked the unused sled. It took her only a couple of minutes to hitch it to the back of the snowmobile. The six-foot bed would haul a prone man.

She didn't let herself think about the situation Oz, Michael, and Nick were in. Her only thoughts were getting there quickly and safely.

"No mistakes," she muttered as she drove the machine over to the women's tent. She checked the carrying box behind the seat. Oz had left the toolbox there, but the emergency kit was gone. They'd brought extra tools, and she ran to the men's tent, located them, and grabbed a couple of blankets off the cots.

As she ran back to the snowmobile, Grant came out of the other tent and handed her the thermos and a flare gun. "There don't seem to be any more flares in here. Maybe in the other tent?"

"I think Oz took them all. You keep that in case something

happens here. Oh, where's the sat phone?"

"I told Oz to keep it. He's already put in a call to Barrow to tell them we need an emergency flight as soon as possible. Charlie said it would be awhile though. He had some minor problem with the chopper, but he was going to fix it first thing in the morning."

Cheryl stared at him. "Is he fixing it now?"

"I think so, but we don't want him hurrying and making a mistake." He smiled bleakly.

"Right." She gulped.

"Just follow the shoreline east. Oz will set off another flare when he hears your engine or sees the headlight of your snowmobile, to mark the spot for you. And be careful. There are ridges and crevices. If you go slowly, it will take you a half hour or so."

"Okay."

"I think you should take one of the heaters."

Cheryl hesitated. They were wasting time, but that could save lives. "All right, get it."

He brought it out, with a spare can of fuel, and secured it on the cargo sled with a bungee cord.

She revved the engine and headed away from camp. At once she felt tiny and alone. The stars glittered overhead, illuminating the endless snowfield. By now she knew the treacheries of the frozen tundra. Instead of running the engine wide open, she had to progress slowly. One advantage was that she knew this first stretch fairly well, and the tracks of other snow machines were easy to see.

"Lord, help me. Get me there safely, so we can bring the others back. And, Lord, please don't let me meet a bear now." Before she could utter an "amen," the eastern sky lit with a fresh orange glow. Adrenaline surged through her, and she hit the throttle.

"Thank You!" She pointed the snow machine's nose toward

the flare. An ice ridge loomed before her, and she tried to slow. The machine hit it, and she flew into the air, clinging to the handgrips. They landed with a crash, and she bounced on the seat but kept her balance. The towed sled thudded behind her. She slowed, thankful to be alive, and looked back. The heater and other gear appeared to be still in place.

"Okay, that was not smart. Thank You, Lord, that I didn't wreck the machine." She took a deep breath, faced forward, eased the throttle in, and continued at a more prudent pace.

Oz and Nick lifted their arms and cheered, waving wildly and hoping she saw them in the glare of the third flare so she wouldn't overshoot their position and hit the same ravine Michael had driven into hours earlier.

Cheryl pulled up and swung around in an arc so that the snowmobile and the cargo sled paralleled their makeshift camp. She killed the engine.

Oz ran to her and pulled her up and into his arms. "Good job, babe! Fantastic!"

She hugged him. "I've got a heater and blankets and coffee. How's Michael doing?"

"Not good. I'm glad you're here." Oz let go of her reluctantly and went to the sled.

"Thanks, Cheryl," Nick called as he rushed to help Oz with the gear.

Michael lay still on a space blanket from one of the emergency kits, near Grant's malfunctioning snowmobile.

Oz brought the heater and set it up beside his prone form.

"Is he conscious?" Cheryl asked.

"No. Hasn't been since the accident, but he's breathing." He tried to downplay his frustration at not being able to do more for Michael.

Grant stood by holding the blankets. "Should I cover him? Maybe we could make a little tent with one of the blankets, to hold heat in."

"I think we should get him back to base camp as soon as possible," Oz said. "Cheryl, are you up to driving him back?"

"Nick should go. He's been out here longest."

"Couldn't we all go at once?" Nick looked from Cheryl to Oz. "Two can ride on the snowmobile. Can't Cheryl sit in the cargo sled with Michael?"

"I don't know if the machine can handle that load," Oz said. "Besides, we don't know what internal injuries Michael has. I think the less we move him the better, and if we lay him flat in the sled, there's no room for anyone else."

"Tell you what," Cheryl said, "I'll stay here with Oz. I brought hot coffee, and we've got the heater now. Nick, you take Michael on the sled. We'll wrap the blankets around him. Take it slow and easy. When you get to camp, Grant will help you get him into the small tent with Annette. Put Michael in my bed—there's no heat in you guys' tent. Then you can stay with Michael and Annette while Grant comes back for Ozzy and me."

"That will work," Nick said.

Oz didn't like that plan. He'd wait with a lot less anxiety if he knew Cheryl was safely back at base camp. He laid a firm hand on her shoulder. "Or you can go with Nick, and I'll just wait here for Grant."

"I'd like to stay." She looked up at him. Her eyes glittered through the holes in her mask. "We'll be perfectly safe now. Grant should be back here in an hour or two."

Oz opened his mouth to discourage her and closed it again. She'd earned the right to decide, and if she wanted to stay out here in the bitter cold for another hour or more, that was her prerogative. And it surely would be more pleasant with her here. "All right then, let's get Michael ready to go."

Cheryl maneuvered the cargo sled as close as she could get it to the injured man. The three of them lifted him on the space blanket and laid him carefully on a woolen one in the sled.

Then they tucked the extra one around him.

"All right, Nick," Oz said. "Be careful."

"We'll be praying for you," Cheryl told him.

"Thanks. And Grant or I will come back as quick as we can for you." He got on the snowmobile and moved out with a jerky start.

Too late, Oz wondered if they should have sent the rookie snowmobiler off on such a crucial mission.

"They'll be okay, as long as he doesn't hurry," Cheryl said.

"I think he's too scared to do that." Oz reached for her hand. "Come on, let's get some of that coffee."

seventeen

The sat together on the seat of Grant's snow machine, facing the heater and taking turns sipping coffee from the plastic cup.

"Did you see the aurora earlier?" Cheryl asked.

"Couldn't miss it."

"It was amazing."

He wrapped his arm around her and slid closer. "I have to admit, I'm glad you're here and I'm not out here alone. I wish you had a more comfortable spot to wait though."

"It's a lot more comfortable than sitting back at camp wondering if you're alive." She winced, wishing she hadn't spoken.

Oz squeezed her gently. "I think I'm starting to understand you. Emotional security is much more important to you than financial or physical security."

She thought about that while he sipped the coffee. "Maybe so. I hadn't really considered it that way."

He handed her the cup, and she swallowed the last bit, which had cooled.

"Do you want some more?" she asked.

"Let's save it awhile."

She nodded. "You know what I've been thinking?"

"What?"

"We should raise the hood on this baby and see if we can get it running."

"Grant and Nick were trying when I got here, but I'm not sure they know as much about engines as you do."

Cheryl stood. "I don't know how many tools they brought along, but I grabbed a few things from the toolbox in your tent before I came."

Oz chuckled. "Why am I not surprised? And here I was wishing we'd brought a dog team instead of snowmobiles."

"We'd all have been home long ago if we were mushing." She switched on her head lamp and flipped up the snow machine's hood.

"Grant thought it was the battery," Oz said, "but the rope start didn't work either."

He opened the carrier behind the seat. "Their tools are in here. Tell me what you need, and I'll hand it to you."

She bent over the task without speaking for several minutes. "Hey, I think I found a loose connection." She turned and chose one of the wrenches he held. "Okay, give it a try."

"Maybe we should pray first."

"Already did, but another prayer wouldn't hurt." She smiled at him then closed her eyes.

"Lord, thank You. . .for everything," Oz said. "We'll leave this up to You."

Cheryl nodded. "Amen." She took the driver's seat and turned the key. The engine sprang to life.

Oz whooped and squeezed her shoulder. "Hallelujah! Now, how are we going to carry the heater?"

"Shut if off and let it cool a few minutes."

"Right. I'll carry it if I have to."

About halfway back to their camp, Oz spotted the light of another snowmobile heading toward them. They met Grant a few minutes later. He waved, circled around, and fell in behind them. Cheryl took them right up to the door of the men's tent, where Oz hopped off and carried the heater inside.

Nick burst in through the doorway. "You got it running." The young scientist's grin covered his whole face. He'd come from the other tent in his flannel shirtsleeves and jeans.

"Not me," Oz told him. "Cheryl did it—totally Cheryl."

Nick whistled softly. "She's quite a lady."

"You got that right." Oz lit the heater and stood to face him.

"You know, sometimes it pays to have a practical person along on the team. So, did you get Michael back here all right?"

"Yes. Grant helped me get him onto the cot. He doesn't look good though. I'd better get back to the other tent and watch him. Annette seems to be okay—she's sawing logs with the best of them. But don't tell her I said that tomorrow, or she'll bite your head off."

Oz smiled. "Cheryl already told me she snores. Doesn't bother me though. I don't have to listen to it."

"Where *is* Cheryl?" Nick asked.

"Probably out helping Grant put the equipment away. I'll go give them a hand."

Cheryl and Grant were just heading for the tents.

"I've got the heater going in the big tent now," Oz said. "You might want to come over to the small one for a while, though, and give it time to warm up." He took the box of gear Cheryl carried, and they went in together.

"So, Nick, what's the story?" Grant asked.

Nick was seated on a stool beside Michael. "Charlie called back and said he'll have a doctor here at sunup. That's not too long now."

Grant nodded. "Sounds good. I suggest we set up a rotation to sit with the patients."

"I'll take the first turn," Cheryl said. "You guys go get a little sleep. I'll come wake one of you in a couple of hours."

"Make it an hour," Oz said, "and wake me first."

"Sounds good to me." Nick rose and reached for his parka.

"It's been a long day for all of us," Grant said.

Oz stopped him before he went out. "Are you two all right? I haven't heard any complaints from you, but if you have any cuts or patches of frostbite, speak up."

"I'm fine, now that I don't have to go out in the cold anymore," Grant said.

Nick threw him an impudent smile. "Well, you have to get

from here to our tent in twenty degrees below zero. But it's not far, Doc. Oh, and I'm fine, too."

"I wish we could do something for Michael," Cheryl said.

Grant went over and stood looking down at the unconscious man. "We checked him over and didn't find any external bleeding. I think he hit his head going down the crevice—he's got a bump—and Annette thought the snow machine may have rolled on him. She was terrified when we got there. I don't see what we can do, other than let him rest quietly." He and Nick exited and fastened down the tent door.

Oz and Cheryl stood looking at each other over the cot where Michael lay. "Feel like praying again?" Oz held out his hand.

She grasped it and bowed her head. Both offered brief, sincere petitions for Michael and Annette. When they'd finished, tears glistened in Cheryl's eyes.

Oz stepped around the foot of the cot and took her in his arms. "You going to be okay?"

"Yes." She sniffed.

"I can sit up with you, and we'll get Nick up after an hour."

"No, go ahead. I'm fine. I'll read a little."

He looked down into her face and brushed back one of her curls. "You are something, you know that? I never know what to expect. You charm bears and engines, and you make the best coffee above the Arctic Circle. And we still have some things to talk about."

"There's time," she whispered.

Oz nodded. "Yes. I'm very thankful for that." He kissed her and let her go.

❧

The sun was barely up the next morning when they heard the beating of the helicopter's rotor. Cheryl hurriedly shoved her feet into her boots and grabbed her parka.

Grant, who was on watch, stirred and looked her way. "I guess Charlie got the chopper fixed."

"Yes. Is anyone else up?"

"I dunno. I've been sitting her since four-thirty. I got a few hours in earlier and thought I'd let the rest have a turn."

"Thanks. I appreciate that. I think I've slept like a log since I crawled into bed." She suspected it was her turn on duty, and Grant had taken pity on her. "I'll go see what's up." She ducked outside.

Oz and Nick emerged from the other tent as the big helicopter swept overhead and settled fifty yards away.

The wash of the wind from the rotors shoved against her, but she could tell the temperature had risen since she'd retired around midnight. She went to stand beside Oz and Nick.

The pilot shut off the engine, and the whirling blades slowed. Charlie and another man got out and walked toward them.

"I'm Dr. Roper. I understand you have a couple of people who need medical attention."

"Right in here, Doctor. Thank you so much for coming." Cheryl led him into the smaller tent. The other men stayed outside, and she could hear Charlie asking if they had breakfast ready.

"Michael is worse off than Annette," she said. "He hasn't regained consciousness since the accident."

Grant moved aside and let the doctor take his seat. He waited with Cheryl while Roper took Michael's vital signs and did a preliminary exam. He turned and asked, "Was either of you there when he fell?"

"No," Grant said. "My assistant and I came along not long after it happened."

Oz stuck his head in the tent doorway and beckoned to Cheryl.

She left Grant to answer the doctor's questions and joined him outside.

"Charlie's willing to fly a couple of us out to the ravine and try to lift Michael's snowmobile out."

"Wouldn't it be dangerous to climb down in there?" Cheryl asked.

"We'd put on a harness. He's got one in the chopper."·

She nodded. "Well, I don't know how long it will take Dr. Roper to get Michael and Annette ready to fly to Barrow."

Charlie wandered over and nodded. "Morning, ma'am."

Oz said, "Nick's gone to the food cache, but I think I'll ask the doctor. Charlie says he can fly us there in ten minutes or so."

Cheryl stared at him. The trip last night had seemed endless. "Is it really that near?"

"I think it's about eight miles. It wouldn't have taken so long if the terrain wasn't so rough."

She nodded. "If you want to ask him, go ahead."

Oz went into the tent and came out in a surprisingly short time. "He says we should wait."

"It's okay," Charlie said. "I'll fly them in to the hospital and come back. You don't want to leave that machine down a crack until it gets snowed on or iced in. Now's the time to salvage it."

Oz nodded. "Thanks, Charlie. We want to retrieve it if we possibly can."

Nick walked quickly toward them between the tents, carrying one of the coolers. "What's the plan?"

Charlie said, "The doc's getting them ready to transport. I'll take them to Barrow and come back for you all."

Nick frowned at Oz. "Are we breaking camp?"

"I don't think so. That is, if you and Grant are willing to continue. We still have five days left. I'd hate to miss out on it."

"Me, too," Nick said.

Cheryl nodded. "I'd like to stay."

"Great," Oz said. "Charlie will come back and help us try to get the snowmobile out of the crevice."

Cheryl looked toward the women's tent. "Maybe we can get Michael's and Annette's gear ready while he's gone. Then Charlie could take their clothes and things to Barrow on his second trip." Cheryl prepared breakfast while the men went over their disorganized gear and helped get Michael into the helicopter.

Annette had awoken. She limped out, leaning on Nick's shoulder, and climbed into the chopper on her own. "If they let me, I'll be back," she called.

Charlie and the physician got in, and they lifted off.

Cheryl stood watching and waving with Oz, Nick, and Grant until the helicopter was only a speck in the sky. Cheryl turned away and noticed that Nick held a plastic grocery bag. "What's that?"

He grinned. "Something I asked Charlie to bring me when I talked to him last night." He opened the bag and pulled out a white bakery box. "I think the coffee's ready. Anybody care for a glazed doughnut?"

"Oh, man!" Oz glared at him. "Don't you know those things are bear magnets?"

Nick's jaw dropped. "I'm sorry. I just thought. . ."

Oz laughed. "I'm kidding. But since there's only four of us now, does that mean we get three apiece?"

❧

Later that morning, all of the scientists and Cheryl flew out to the scene of the accident. Charlie had brought his son along. It seemed the young man, Barney, was always ready for adventure. The others watched from the ground as his father hovered and lowered Barney down to the disabled snow machine.

Rather than a crevasse in a glacier, the declivity was more of a steep-sided ravine in the tundra. The snowmobile lay upside down. Barney attached two cables to it, unclipped his harness, and stood back. Charlie raised the machine slowly and swung it out onto the level ground where Oz unhooked it. Then he flew back out over the ravine, and Barney clipped on and rode up to join them. He arrived on solid ground clutching a camera, a zippered survival kit, and a clipboard.

"Hey, fantastic!" Grant took the things from his arms, and Barney unfastened the cable. "Is there anything else down there that we can get?"

"Yeah, did you see a satellite phone by any chance?" Oz asked. "Those things are very expensive."

Barney shook his head. "This is everything I saw, but there could be other things scattered further down."

By the time Charlie landed the chopper again and walked over to them, the men had righted the snowmobile. The windshield sported a long crack, but the keys were still in the ignition.

Cheryl tried to start it, but the engine wouldn't catch.

"Too bad," Grant said.

"Aw, don't give up so easily." Cheryl grinned at him. "We brought a can of fuel, didn't we?"

"You think it's just out of gas?"

She shrugged. "The engine was running when Michael barreled over the edge, and the key was still in the on position. They must have been getting low anyway at the end of the day. I'm thinking it ran for a little while and then quit. It was upside down, after all."

Barney ran to the chopper for the gas can and poured the contents into the snowmobile's tank.

Cheryl turned the key again. The engine roared.

"Hey, lady! Good job!" Grant high-fived her.

Oz laughed. "I told you she's something!"

Cheryl put it in gear and let it run forward a few feet, then stopped it. She yelled, "The chassis is pretty beat up, but I think I can drive it back to camp."

"I'll come with you." Oz climbed on behind her.

"All right," Grant said. "We'll see you back at camp. I'm going to see if Charlie and his son are willing to make one more try at finding that sat phone."

"If Barney doesn't want to go down again, I'm willing to try," Nick said.

"Okay, you guys sort it out," Oz said. "Oh, wait a sec. I brought the dart rifle. It's in the chopper. I'd better grab it, just in case." He ran to the helicopter and got the gun. Once he was seated again behind Cheryl, he waved to the four men. "See you later."

Cheryl drove the damaged snowmobile slowly. He didn't really need to hold on to her, but he wanted to, so he rode with his arms around her waist all the way back to base camp. There was no sign of the helicopter, so Oz assumed Charlie and Barney had agreed to go fishing again in the ravine.

As they puttered toward the camp, Cheryl suddenly backed off on the throttle and stopped their progress. "Oh, great! Just what we needed."

Oz stared toward the camp. The larger tent lay in a heap. In the middle of it sat a white bear, licking a cardboard box.

"Man! I *told* Nick not to leave those extra doughnuts lying around."

Cheryl looked over her shoulder at him. "Look at it this way—you don't have to chase around all afternoon to find a bear."

"Right you are. Do you want to shoot this one?" He hefted the dart gun.

"Don't mind if I do." She reached for the weapon. "One of those doughnuts was mine."

eighteen

While the men put their tent to rights, Cheryl went over the snow machine again. The fiberglass engine cover had taken quite a beating, but the mechanical parts seemed none the worse.

The large tent was up again. She walked over and called to Oz, "So, he didn't tear the tent to shreds?"

"Apparently he swiped the door open and just walked right in. There are a couple of slices in the ceiling. That's probably where he fought his way out. But I think we can fix it. There's an extra awning we haven't been using, and we can use it for patching."

"Sounds like a good day's work."

"Probably so. I don't think he'd been here long when we arrived. Otherwise, he'd have done more damage." He smiled at her. "I'm glad he was happy to leave when we let him wake up."

"I'm sure the roaring monster that chased him away had something to do with that."

"Yeah, helicopters do have their good points, don't they?"

"Yes, I have to admit, we probably wouldn't have found the satellite phone if Charlie and Barney hadn't helped us out with the chopper. I just hope that greedy bear doesn't come back." She spotted the camp stove sitting outside the tent. "So, is the stove workable?"

"Sure. Are you in the cooking mood?"

"I don't know. Those doughnuts are sitting kind of heavy."

Oz pulled her to him. "Sometime I'm going to hug you when we're not both wearing Arctic gear. But you know what? There's no one I'd rather be in a rough spot with than you."

❧

Five days later they walked together out of security at the Ted

Stevens Anchorage Airport and strolled hand in hand toward baggage claim. As they came down the escalator, Cheryl stiffened. "There they are!" She began walking down the steps to get to her family faster.

Steve, Rick, and Robyn clustered about them for hugs and handshakes. Everyone talked at once as they ambled toward the baggage carousels.

"Mom, are you sure you're okay?" Robyn asked.

"Yes. I told you on the phone that we're both fine."

"I know, but we saw pictures on the news the other night of a helicopter pulling that snow machine out of the hole—"

"Honey, Oz and I weren't on it when it crashed. We were miles away."

"I know, but then they showed you doing something to a very lethargic polar bear."

Cheryl laughed. "Oz let me tattoo that sucker's tag number on his lip. He ate my doughnut, and I wanted revenge."

Robyn turned to her husband with a helpless stare. "I've never seen her like this before."

Oz laughed and put his arm around Cheryl. "Your mother is an amazing woman. Wait until you hear all the things she did in the last two weeks."

"Well, I want to see the gun you used to drug those bears," Steve said.

Rick held up his hands. "Hold on, folks. Let's collect the luggage and go get something to eat. I'm sure Cheryl and Ozzy would like to have dinner in a nice restaurant."

"Would we ever," Oz said. "And I don't care if I never see another granola bar again as long as I live."

"He's rather partial to ham sandwiches though," Cheryl said with a smirk.

❧

Oz drove to the Hollands' house at eleven the next morning. He and Cheryl had been ordered by Rick to take a day off and get some rest before they returned to work. But Oz couldn't relax, knowing he had unfinished business.

Cheryl came to the door wearing corduroy pants and a faded flannel shirt over a black T-shirt. "Ozzy. Come in."

He stepped inside and looked around for Grandpa Steve. "Where's Mr. Holland?"

"He's out back with Robyn, in the dog yard."

"Oh."

"I didn't expect to see you today. Would you like some coffee?"

"Sure, if it's no trouble."

"Not a bit."

He let her hang up his coat and followed her to the kitchen. As she got out mugs, he perched on a high stool beside her work island. "I woke up early this morning and couldn't go back to sleep."

"Not me," she said. "I just got up about an hour ago. That mattress felt *so* good."

"I, uh. . .drove in to Anchorage."

She turned and cocked an eyebrow at him. "You went to Anchorage this morning? We just came from there last night."

"I know, but there was something I wanted to do."

She stamped her foot in mock frustration. "Did you go to Title Wave without me?"

He laughed. "No, if I'm heading for the bookstore, I'll be sure and invite you along."

"Good. So what were you up to?"

He reached into his pocket and drew out a small wooden box and placed it on the counter.

"What's this?"

"Open it."

She eyed him suspiciously. "Ozzy? What did you do?"

She was going to make him work hard, he could see that. He left the stool and walked over to stand beside her. Looking down into her eyes, just the color of coffee the way he liked it, set his pulse pounding. "Cheryl, I. . ."

Something in her expression softened. She was no longer teasing him. Her mouth twitched, and she waited, eyes full of questions, but not in a hurry.

He cleared his throat and went down on one knee, reaching for her hand. "I feel as though God brought us together. Not Rick, not the job. It's meant to be. Cheryl, I love you. And I love Alaska. I want to stay here and share it with you. Please, will you marry me?"

One tear escaped her eyelid and rolled down her cheek. "Of course," she whispered.

He considered making a wisecrack about how glad his achy knees were that she hadn't kept him waiting. Instead, he pushed himself to his feet and hauled her into his embrace. He hadn't kissed her nearly enough when the back door rattled.

The two of them sprang apart. Cheryl's face was red as she turned to face Robyn and Steve. Oz wondered if he looked as guilty.

"Hey, Mom. Hello, Ozzy," Robyn said uncertainly.

"Hi, honey. Come on in. We were just going to have some coffee."

Grandpa Steve chortled. "Oh, so that's what you call it now."

Oz couldn't help grinning.

Robyn stepped over to the work island and picked up the tiny wooden box. "What's this?"

"Uh. . ." Cheryl threw him a panicky glance.

"It's something I bought in Anchorage," Oz said. "Open it and tell me what you think."

Robyn raised her eyebrows and glanced at her mother, but Cheryl turned her back and reached for the coffeepot. Robyn sprang the clasp and gasped. "Oh! That is so. . .gorgeous. Mom?"

"It's Alaska jade and gold, isn't it?" Steve asked.

"Yes," Oz said. "I thought it was pretty myself and should be worn by a beautiful woman."

"Mom?" Robyn walked deliberately around her mother and faced her. "Look at me, Mother."

Slowly Cheryl raised her gaze to Robyn's. Her daughter searched her face eagerly.

Cheryl looked down at the box in Robyn's hand. Another tear rolled down her cheek. She looked over at Oz. "It's beautiful. Thank you."

"Seems to me this calls for a celebration," Steve said.

"Uh, that's what we were doing when you walked in," Oz said.

Robyn laughed. "Then, by all means, carry on. Come on, Grandpa. Let's go in the other room and call Rick. He ought to come over for lunch if he can get away from the office and help us all celebrate. Then we'll run to the store and buy an ice cream cake."

"You don't need to do that," Cheryl said quickly. "I mean, you can stay for lunch if you want, but... On second thought, I don't think I have anything to feed you. I need to get some groceries into the house. I can make cheese sandwiches, maybe."

Robyn threw her arms around her mother. "No. Don't cook anything. Grandpa and I will go over to my house. I'll fix lunch for all of us over there. You and Ozzy come over when you're ready. Not too soon though. Take your time." She let go of her mother and propelled Steve toward the back door as she spoke.

"Hey, wait," Steve said. "I want to know if this means they're getting married. I mean, that there is a serious rock."

Robyn stopped, and they both looked at Oz and Cheryl.

Oz waited for her to speak.

A slow smile curved Cheryl's lips. "Yes, it most certainly does."

epilogue

A month later, Cheryl and Oz took their vows in the church in Wasilla. Oz had already submitted their grant application for a longer research trip to the North Slope the following spring. To his surprise, Cheryl had insisted he ask for the use of a helicopter during the entire expedition.

Several of Oz's former colleagues had flown to Alaska for the wedding. He suspected some of them used it as an excuse to travel on afterward and ogle the state's bears.

Rick stood beside him at the front of the church. When the music began, Robyn came down the aisle first, resplendent in a shimmery green dress, the color of the stone in the ring Oz had given Cheryl. With her hair bound up in a delicate twist sprigged with flowers, Robyn looked more feminine than Oz had ever seen her. Rick's eyes sparkled as he watched her. In the front pew, Aven and Caddie juggled little Axel back and forth between them.

The cadence changed, and Oz looked toward the entrance. Cheryl entered on her father-in-law's arm. Her eyes sought him, and his heart lurched. Absolutely beautiful. No sad memories beleaguered him. When she placed her hand in his, he knew they could conquer any differences that came up.

They drove as far as Anchorage that evening. Oz called the charter airline from their hotel room, to make sure all was well for their flight to Kodiak the next day.

When he hung up, he joined Cheryl at the window, where she stood looking out at the Chugach Mountains. He slid his arms around her. "Last chance to change your mind and take the ferry instead of flying."

She shook her head. "It would take too long. We'll be fine. Flying doesn't—"

"I know. Flying doesn't bother you."

"Right." She bounced up on her toes and kissed him. "I'm just surprised you didn't insist on a honeymoon in the tropics."

"No, Kodiak is perfect. Your son lives there. . ."

"Yes, I've always wanted to see it. Of course, Aven and Caddie will still be in Wasilla. . ."

"I'm told it's one of the most beautiful places on earth."

"I've heard that. And—oh—did you know?" She smiled mischievously. "They have bears, too."

"Seems like someone mentioned that to me."

She nodded and ran her hands through his hair. "All in all, I thought it was the perfect destination."

A Letter To Our Readers

Dear Reader:

In order that we might better contribute to your reading enjoyment, we would appreciate your taking a few minutes to respond to the following questions. We welcome your comments and read each form and letter we receive. When completed, please return to the following:

Fiction Editor
Heartsong Presents
PO Box 719
Uhrichsville, Ohio 44683

1. Did you enjoy reading *Polar Opposites* by Susan Page Davis?
   ❑ Very much! I would like to see more books by this author!
   ❑ Moderately. I would have enjoyed it more if

   _____

   _____

   _____

2. Are you a member of **Heartsong Presents**? ❑ Yes ❑ No
   If no, where did you purchase this book? _____

   _____

3. How would you rate, on a scale from 1 (poor) to 5 (superior), the cover design? _____

4. On a scale from 1 (poor) to 10 (superior), please rate the following elements.

   _____ Heroine   _____ Plot
   _____ Hero   _____ Inspirational theme
   _____ Setting   _____ Secondary characters

5. These characters were special because? _____
_____
_____

6. How has this book inspired your life? _____
_____
_____

7. What settings would you like to see covered in future
   Heartsong Presents books? _____
   _____
   _____

8. What are some inspirational themes you would like to see
   treated in future books? _____
   _____
   _____

9. Would you be interested in reading other **Heartsong
   Presents** titles? ❏ Yes ❏ No

10. Please check your age range:
    ❏ Under 18   ❏ 18-24
    ❏ 25-34   ❏ 35-45
    ❏ 46-55   ❏ Over 55

Name _____
Occupation _____
Address _____
City, State, Zip _____
E-mail _____

MAINELY
MYSTERIES

3 stories in 1

It's mainly moonlight, mayhem, and murder in small-town Maine.

Suspense, paperback, 480 pages, 5¾6" x 8 "

Hearts♥ng

Any 12
Heartsong
Presents titles
for only
$27.00*

CONTEMPORARY ROMANCE IS CHEAPER BY THE DOZEN!

Buy any assortment of twelve *Heartsong Presents* titles and save 25% off the already discounted price of $2.97 each!

*plus $4.00 shipping and handling per order and sales tax where applicable.
If outside the U.S. please call
740-922-7280 for shipping charges.

HEARTSONG PRESENTS TITLES AVAILABLE NOW:

(If ordering from this page, please remember to include it with the order form.)

Presents

___HP790 *Garlic and Roses*, G. Martin
___HP793 *Coming Home*, T. Fowler
___HP794 *John's Quest*, C. Dowdy
___HP797 *Building Dreams*, K. Y'Barbo
___HP798 *Courting Disaster*, A. Boeshaar
___HP801 *Picture This*, N. Farrier
___HP802 *In Pursuit of Peace*, J. Johnson
___HP805 *Only Today*, J. Odell
___HP806 *Out of the Blue*, J. Thompson
___HP809 *Suited for Love*, L.A. Coleman
___HP810 *Butterfly Trees*, G. Martin
___HP813 *Castles in the Air*, A. Higman and
          J. A. Thompson
___HP814 *The Preacher Wore a Gun*, J. Livingston
___HP817 *By the Beckoning Sea*, C. G. Page
___HP818 *Buffalo Gal*, M. Connealy
___HP821 *Clueless Cowboy*, M. Connealy
___HP822 *Walk with Me*, B. Melby and C. Wienke
___HP825 *Until Tomorrow*, J. Odell
___HP826 *Milk Money*, C. Dowdy
___HP829 *Leap of Faith*, K. O'Brien
___HP830 *The Bossy Bridegroom*, M. Connealy
___HP833 *To Love a Gentle Stranger*, C. G. Page
___HP834 *Salt Water Taffie*, J. Hanna
___HP837 *Dream Chasers*, B. Melby and C. Wienke
___HP838 *For the Love of Books*, D. R. Robinson
___HP841 *Val's Prayer*, T. Fowler
___HP842 *The Superheroes Next Door*, A Boeshaar
___HP845 *Cotton Candy Clouds*, J. Hanna

___HP846 *Bittersweet Memories*, C. Dowdy
___HP849 *Sweet Joy of My Life*, C. G. Page
___HP850 *Trail to Justice*, S. P. Davis
___HP853 *A Whole New Light*, K. O'Brien
___HP854 *Hearts on the Road*, D. Brandmeyer
___HP857 *Stillwater Promise*, B. Melby and
          C. Wienke
___HP858 *A Wagonload of Trouble*, V. McDonough
___HP861 *Sweet Harmony*, J. Hanna
___HP862 *Heath's Choice*, T. Fowler
___HP865 *Always Ready*, S. P. Davis
___HP866 *Finding Home*, J. Johnson
___HP869 *Noah's Ark* , D. Mayne
___HP870 *God Gave the Song*, K.E. Kovach
___HP873 *Autumn Rains*, M. Johnson
___HP874 *Pleasant Surprises*, B. Melby &
          C. Wienke
___HP877 *A Still, Small Voice*, K. O'Brein
___HP878 *Opie's Challenge*, T. Fowler
___HP881 *Fire and Ice*, S. P. Davis
___HP882 *For Better or Worse*, J. Johnson
___HP885 *A Hero for Her Heart*, C. Speare &
          N. Toback
___HP886 *Romance by the Book*, M. Johnson
___HP889 *Special Mission*, D. Mayne
___HP890 *Love's Winding Path*, L. Bliss
___HP893 *Disarming Andi*, E. Goddard
___HP894 *Crossroads Bay*, K. Kovach

Great Inspirational Romance at a Great Price!

Heartsong Presents books are inspirational romances in contemporary and historical settings, designed to give you an enjoyable, spirit-lifting reading experience. You can choose wonderfully written titles from some of today's best authors like Wanda E. Brunstetter, Mary Connealy, Susan Page Davis, Cathy Marie Hake, Joyce Livingston, and many others.

When ordering quantities less than twelve, above titles are $2.97 each.
Not all titles may be available at time of order.